On The Edge: New Women'

G000128414

Chick-Luv

On The Edge: New Women's Fiction Anthology

Chick-Lit 2

(*No Chick Vics*)

**edited by
Cris Mazza
Jeffrey DeShell
Elisabeth Sheffield**

**editorial assistants
Glynis Kinnan
Lily James
Lisa Stolley**

Normal

Published by FC2 with support given by the English Department Unit
for Contemporary Literature of Illinois State University, the Illinois
Arts Council, and the National Endowment for the Arts.

Address all inquiries to: FC2, Unit for Contemporary Literature,
Campus Box 4241, Illinois State University, Normal, IL 61790-4241

On the Edge: New Women's Fiction Anthology
Chick-Lit 2: (No Chick Vics)
Cris Mazza

ISBN: Paper: 1-57366-020-5

Book design: David Dean
Cover design: Todd Bushman
Cover art: Rikki Ducornet

Produced and printed in the United States of America

 This program is
partially supported by
a grant from the
Illinois Arts Council.

 NATIONAL
ENDOWMENT
FOR THE
ARTS

Chick-Lit 2

Table of Contents

Notes & Commentary
from the Editors

Notes and Commentary
from the editors

Cris Mazza
Jeffrey DeShell
Elisabeth Sheffield

Betty and The Boys

Once in a town. There was a little girl named Betty. She lived with her mother, and her brother, Near there was Some boys. They Didn't like girls. So they ran when they Saw girls. Sometimes. they hit the girls.
There was one girl tht

hit Boys. Her name was Betty, Her Brother played With the boys, One day Betty, told her mother, Her mother

told the Boys mother. the Boys
mother Told the Boys to Stop
girls. Or Betty won't Stop
Hiting you and from then
after the Boys and girls
Played whith ehather.
and thay played like
That for eaver.
and that is
how it was.

short story by Cris Mazza
age 7

No Victims, the anti-theme

What is a *theme* anthology? Frankly, its theme is a marketing tool. Just saying, "This is a remarkable collection of stories," isn't always quite enough to sell a book, either to an individual reader or prospective publisher. On the other hand, say "Here's a book of great new stories *about* _____," and you've automatically got a hook ... and, hopefully, a ready-made audience, created out of a pre-existing camp. Love-gone-wrong, change-of-life, single parenthood, losing a baby, adoption, physical handicaps, attachments to pets, relationships with food or drugs or alcohol, abusive relationships, regional lifestyles, favorite childhood toys. Collections of stories have acquired the necessity of being about something, proving something, illustrating something, exploring something ... one *thing*, a SUBJECT.

The theme possibilities could be limitless. However, perhaps with the growth of publicity-via-confessional, on talk shows, tabloid news and other media—Roseanne a casualty of parental abuse, Carroll O'Connor's son driven to suicide by drugs —a prevailing type of theme anthology is a victim theme, usually a victim-and-recovery theme: sharing the trauma but providing a glimmer of hope, an inspiration, a feel-good reason for grouping together stories about certain types of personal and/or intimate tragedies.

Let me stop right now and say:
YES, THEY ARE ALL TRAGIC, UNDESERVED AFFLICTIONS AND ALL POINT TO SOMETHING GONE TERRIBLY WRONG WITH HUMAN SOCIETY !

Since FC2 is a publisher of non-commercial fiction, it certainly wouldn't seem apt to do an anthology with a selling hook, especially a popular one, no matter how noble the editorial motivation for choosing the particular victimization as a motif. So an anti-theme anthology seemed an obvious choice. However, a true anti-theme anthology is *not* necessarily just one without any theme at al —that un-salable book of great stories—but could also be one that explores those fictions which don't seem to fit the favorite, marketable anthology themes. Thus NO VICTIMS.

Well, that's one excuse for this book.

Actually, there's a more seriously contemplated reason for the theme NO VICTIMS.

It's true that our *Chick-Lit 2* theme did originate from a growing awareness of the large number of theme anthologies involving victim subjects—rape survivors, addictions of all kinds, parental abuse, individuals emotionally debilitated by a particular religion, incest, sexual harassment. Similarly, in reading the 400 submissions to *Chick-Lit* in 1994, we found that stories about women as victims is a popular trend for women writers. Is this trend *bad* or *wrong*? Not at all. Go ahead and continue to attempt to wake the world from its complacent slumber.

BUT...

From the CHICK-LIT 2 rejection letter.
When I proposed the theme NO VICTIMS for the 2nd *Chick-Lit* anthology, what I meant was: while we're looking for new or alternative voices in women's fiction, let's also look for story content without a trauma that comes from *outside* the character — unfortunate perpetrations like incest or sexual assault or the disease of addiction, caused not by an individual's choice or motive but by anything from neglectful parents to a patriarchal society to poverty to media to government to money & power all being in the hands of men (oh, I guess that's the same as patriarchal society) — things beyond the character's control which can then be blamed for the aftermath the victim is left to deal with.

No I Didn't Mean 'They' Ask To Be Raped / Harassed / Molested ! Sexual assaults and harassments and injurious poor body images *do* exist and have waged a war on women (the American Medical Association says so too). But for this book, I was interested in seeing what action(s) women [characters] can incite *on their own*, whether bad or good, hopeful or dead-end, progressive or destructive. We [the editors] hope that women aren't *only* what society has made them and that there is *some* individual identity to work with.

In victim-fiction, a perfectly nice, promising person encounters *IT*. Incest, rape, mugging, sexual harassment, drug/alcohol addiction, sexual discrimination. The now-victim then begins to struggle with the *AFTERMATH*. Eating disorders, more addictions, self mutilation, low self esteem, dangerous passivity that allows further harassment or abuse. And that's the story's movement/intensity.

Sample of the typical cover letter we received:
Please consider my story for your "No Victims" anthology. Although the 16-year-old narrator is a victim of _____, she gains strength and breaks the cycle of abuse.

I suspect the troubled industry is subtly driving writers to use what has already proven to be moving material. If so, how about, just for this book if you want, instead of a fiction's drama beginning and developing because of something that happens—randomly, through fate or a fucked-up society—*to* someone, therefore creating an "inner conflict" which will then "develop," how about fiction by & about women where the movement or tension or intensity stems *primarily* from who a character is and what she wants. So OK, sometimes she'll still end up a victim, but the story itself isn't based on a thunderbolt from the blue targeting an innocent someone and determining the course of their future emotional duress or social difficulties or personal obstacles.

In my novel *Your Name Here: _____*, a character has unconsentual sex as a partial result of "acting out" blindly—out of retaliation, resentment and anger, out of wanting revenge for unrequited feelings. I intended for her to be a victim, but not simply a victim of male society that rapes its women, but of something more subtle (and more dangerous): a victim of whatever causes her to ignore the intellect she's been given, ignore the education she has, ignore the fact that she has a job she's good at, and be guided *only* by wanting a man to think of her as attractive, desirable, a potential sex partner. A goal more important than career or accomplishment. A goal that supersedes all other noble pursuits. And few women even realize they're doing it. No one forces women to do this. Perhaps that "evil" "society" encourages it, implants it, but if we're, by now, smart enough to recognize it, aren't we also smart enough to resist it? If not—*THAT'S* scary.

And yet, you'll find some of the classic trappings of victimhood here—self mutilation, S&M pornography, non-mutual sexual experiences—but there's a difference. These aren't stories about the traumas of, aftermath of and recovering from victimhood. In fact, *certain writers don't seem to consider victimizing situations as victimizing, and the victims don't regard themselves as victims at all!*
Could this be a symptom of postfeminist writing?

From the original call-for-manuscripts for CHICK-LIT in 1994:

What is *Postfeminist* Writing?

If you have no answer or don't even know what the question means ... *good*, perhaps *you're* a postfeminist writer. Just another absurd label, but it—like *all* labels—represents contemporary criticism's on-going quest to locate, define and thereby understand writers who, for reasons as individual as they are, haven't been embraced or appreciated.

When the first On The Edge: New Women's Fiction Anthology was released in October 1995, my ice-breaker, aren't-I-funny-as-shit identification tag in the call-for-manuscripts had become the subtitle:

Chick-Lit: Postfeminist Fiction

There was even a colon! All of a sudden I was *responsible* for something, expected to define and defend it, wear the plaque, lead the garrison. Trying to remain undaunted, I offered a complimentary copy to a senior faculty member in English and Women's Studies. "Postfeminist, huh? What's that? Hope you're not implying all the issues have been solved or are obsolete."

My abashed response:
No.

But then someone else said it better ....

> ONE GENERATION OF WOMEN WROTE "SHIT HAPPENS."
> THE NEXT SAYS, "YEAH, IT STILL DOES,
> BUT I'VE STUCK MY FINGERS IN IT."

2 girls review

—Cris Mazza

"She wanted to die, but she also wanted to live in Paris."
On Being the Male Editor of a Feminist Anthology
Part II

Naming the Victims. Please identify the heroine in Column I
with the appropriate text in Column II. Then indicate in
Column III whether she is a Victim or Not. Authors' names
are in parentheses, and "answers" are at the bottom.

I	II	III
1) Emma Bovary (Gustave Flaubert)	a) All of the whores agreed with O: it was the end of the white world.	Victim/Not Victim
2) Floria Tusca (Music by G. Puccini, libretto by Illica & Giacosa)	b) "I want to be the girl with the most cake."	Victim/Not Victim
3) Robin Vote (Djuna Barnes)	c) Should you ever find my domination unendurable and should your chains ever become too heavy, you will be obliged to kill yourself, for I will never set you free.	Victim/Not Victim
4) Dolores Haze (Vladimir Nabokov)	d) She will not tell Champ that her first fuck was a guy named Puppet who ejaculated prematurely, at the sight of her apricot vagina, so plump and fuzzy.—Pendejo—she said—you got it all over me. She rubbed the gooey substance off	Victim/Not Victim

her legs, her belly, in disgust. Ran home to tell Rat and Pancha, her mouth open with laughter.

5) Margarite (J.W. von Goethe)	e) I stayed there, staring at myself in the glass. What do I want to cry about?...On the contrary, it's when I am quite sane like this, when I have had a couple of drinks and am quite sane, that I realize how lucky I am. Saved, rescued, fished-up, half-drowned, out of the deep dark river, dry clothes, hair shampooed and set. Nobody would know I had ever been in it. Except, of course, that there always remains something. Yes, there always remains something.	Victim/Not Victim
6) Courtney Love	f) "Why d'ya do it?" she said "Why d'ya spit on my snatch "Are we out of love now? Is this just a bad patch?"	Victim/Not Victim
7) Miss Williams (Paule Marshall)	g) Let him know the sacrifice Which I made for love For the very last breath of life— Will be for him alone.	Victim/Not Victim
8) Maria Braun (Rainer Werner Fassbinder)	h) The sound of her breathing, which had grown louder, might have give the illusion of the panting of sexual pleasure, and when mine was at its climax, I could kiss her without having interrupted her sleep. I felt at such moments I had possessed her more completely, like an unconscious and unresisting object of dumb nature.	Victim/Not Victim

9) The narrator (M a r g u e r i t e Duras)	i) "You mean," she persisted, now kneeling above me, "you never did it when you were a kid?" "Never," I answered quite truthfully. "Okay," said [she], "here is where we start."	Victim/Not Victim
10) Sethe (Toni Morrison)	j) I lived for art. I lived for love: Never did I harm a living creature! Whatever misfortunes I encountered I sought with secret hand to succor Even in pure faith, My prayers rose In the Holy Chapels, Even in pure faith I brought flowers to the altars In this hour of pain, why, why Oh Lord Why dost thou repay me thus?	Victim/Not Victim
11) Patti Smith	k) She used to keep her pigeons in the loft above the disused stable and feed them grain out of the palms of her cupped hands. She liked to feel the soft scratch of their little beaks. They murmured "vroo croo" with infinite tenderness. She changed their water every day and cleaned up their leprous messes but Old Borden took a dislike to their cooing, it got on his nerves— who'd have thought the *had* any nerves? But he invented some, they got on them, and one afternoon he took out the hatchet from the wood-pile in the cellar and chopped the pigeons' heads off.	Victim/Not Victim
12) Violetta Valéry (Music by G. Verdi, libretto by F.M. Piave	l) "My dear…, I assure you I was not attracted to you because you were colored…" And he broke off, remembering just how acutely aware of her color he had been.	Victim/Not Victim

13) Auntie V (Marianne Hauser)	m) "She wanted to die, but she also wanted to live in Paris."	Victim/Not Victim
14) Lizzie Borden (Angela Carter)	n) "Jesus died for somebody's sins—but not mine."	Victim/Not Victim
15) Wanda von Sacher-Masoch	o) No, no, you must outlive us! Here is what manner of graves to give us, I charge you, go to it, Tomorrow do it. The best place give to my mother, Right next to her put my brother, And me at a distance, pray, But not too far away! And the little one by my right breast. There's no one else will lie by me!	Victim/Not Victim
16) Albertine (Marchel Proust)	p) Inside, two boys bled in the saw-dust and dirt at the feet of a nigger woman holding a blood-soaked child to her child with one hand and an infant by the heels in another. She did not look at them; she simply swung the baby toward the wall planks, missed and tried to connect a second time.	Victim/Not Victim
17) Marianne Faithfull	q) And the girl started up as if to go and kill herself in her turn, throw herself in her turn into the sea, and afterwards she wept because she thought of the man from Cholon and suddenly she wasn't sure if she had loved him with a love she hadn't seen because it had lost itself in the affair like water in sand and she	Victim/Not Victim

rediscovered it only now, through
this moment of music flung across
the sea.

18) The narrator (Kathy Acker)	r) Then she began to bark also, crawling after him—barking in a fit of laughter, obscene and touching. The dog began to cry then, running with her, head-on with her head, as if to circumvent her: soft and slow his feet went padding. He ran this way and that low down in his throat crying, and she grinning and crying with him; crying in shorter and shorter spaces, moving head to head, until she gave up, lying out, her hands beside her, her face turned and weeping.	Victim/Not Victim
19) Sasha (Jean Rhys)	s) When I explore you with my tongue I make love to your female lovers, my jealousy becomes flesh. I make my jealousy work for me tooth and nail, tongue, nipples, knees and thumb all the way up the old ladder of ecstasy until my clitoris screams in a frenzy. Yes, J, each woman you've had in the flesh I've had in my mind.	Victim/Not Victim
20) Arlene (Helena María Viramontes)	t) "I don't wait for miracles—I prefer making them."	Victim/Not Victim

Answers: 1 - m, 2 - j, 3 - r, 4 - i, 5 - o, 6 - b, 7 - l, 8 - t, 9 - q, 10 - p, 11 - n, 12 - g, 13 - s, 14 - k, 15 - c, 16 - h, 17 - f, 18 - a, 19 - e, 20 - d.

—Jeffrey DeShell

Borders of the Abyss

"No victims." I'm going to begin by admitting that the phrase makes me uncomfortable. It's pre-emptive and coldly commanding, like "No Smoking" or "No Dogs" or "No Shoes, No Shirt, No Service." Such phrases withdraw any specific authority (who says "No Smoking"?), and thus evoke all authority. When I was kid they made me feel like lighting up, letting my dog take a dump on the courthouse lawn, putting my bare feet up on the lunch counter. Now I'm posting signs myself—"Victims Keep Out." And further, there's the problem that signs create borders which must then be patrolled. No admittance, then, to the story about the thirteen year old girl raped by her favorite uncle, or the one about the woman whose boss offers her a forty cent per hour raise for a little "overtime" at the office, or about the village where clitoridectomies are a venerable tradition (unless, of course, the writer has somehow subverted the position of the "victim," by allowing her to initiate or somehow redefine the act of violence). With my arms crossed over the front of my leather jacket, tapping the toes of my shiny black boots, I coolly size these heart wrenching experiences up and send them away.

How callous to dismiss such stories, when so often they are true—at least in terms of the overall, statistically measurable reality they refer to. This is undeniably a world where women are molested, beaten, raped, overworked and underpaid more often than men. In asking for stories without victims, haven't we, the editors of this collection, chosen to ignore this world? Maybe, maybe not—it depends on how one looks at it. Think, for example of the image of a girl who cuts herself, over and over, so that there are "wounds talking at the shoulder, at the bicep, at the collarbone opening and closing their little red lips." I can look at this image and think, how sad: she's crying out for help, having been driven insane by a society which urges women to starve and torture their bodies in the quest of beauty. On the other hand, it's possible to see this as "a violence that opens up the world to a difference," a violence that takes the images projected at us by the media and the eyes of others, and *creatively* refigures and reworks them into something as unrecognizable as a way out.

The quotations in the paragraph above, by the way, are taken from Lidia Yuknavitch's *Loving dora*, which is a revision of Freud's *Dora: An Analysis of a Case of Hysteria*. As a creative writing teacher and an editor of this collection, I've seen several other attempts to rewrite this text (which has become standard fare in feminist theory courses). All of these focused on more or less the same theme: that Freud coaxed poor Dora's story away from her, then pried it open and shafted it. Historically, the theme of the seducer who has his way with an innocent woman is a useful one: in the novel, it has served to shore up male potency and power, female innocence and inculpability. In other words, it has reinforced the gender oppositions that even now, in the late 20th century, define and limit a person's psyche. Thus when Dora's mother, the passive, pill-popping housewife, gazes into a polished spoon, it "reflects back at her the only image she could ever be."

New images won't, of course, lower male testosterone levels or increase female bone mass. And certainly it is debatable whether creative self-mutilation could be a kind of empowerment. On the other hand, the "reality" that we possess, a reality of female victimization, is not reducible to facts such as the greater strength and power of human males (consider, for instance, the rarity of rape amongst other animal species). Our reality is a creation of ideology, which determines both the images we choose and what we make these images "mean." One can write as if the category of "woman" (or "man") is an absolute. Or one can acknowledge that it is what Diane Elam calls "a mise en abyme, a structure of infinite deferral." Within the abyss, "there are established, preconceived notions of what women can be and do, and at the same time 'women' remains a yet to be determined category." To imagine such a structure, consider the image of a woman gazing into spoon. Inside the spoon is another woman gazing into a spoon, and inside that spoon is another woman gazing into a spoon.... Or imagine a woman holding a mirror up to her sex, examining the secret folds of her desire...

And maybe what she sees in the mirror is Tristan Taormino's woman "covered in blue saran wrap" who "must be suffocating" as a "young alternative rockerboy" looks on, while a man photographs them both, capturing the jewel case cliché. But beyond this image is another of a woman in a baby doll dress, being fingered by a second woman, who is in turn watching a third woman, a "live girl" dancing on stage: "She slides back my wet panties, can't take her eyes off the girl, can't take her hands off me." And within this image is one of the woman (the same woman as in scenes I and II?) with another two women, one of whom is telling her "how fuckable her ass is." As if to satisfy the desire for the phallus evoked in the previous image, in the next image the woman's female lover has a "dick." But now, perhaps, the abyss is becoming overly determined; now possibly, the images of the woman are crystallizing into one: lesbian, "femme," "bottom." Thus in the next image, the woman has tied a man to a chair, gagged and strapped him. She's whipping him because "he's asking for it," because she's "high from fucking this motherfucker and if someone yelled cut or stop, I didn't hear it." And so on...

I referred above to the violence that could make a difference, leading to something as unrecognizable as a way out. Probably cutting up one's body to make it non-representational, or playing "bottom" with women and "top" with men, won't get us out of the abyss that is "woman." On the other hand, as Elam writes, not only does each additional image change "all the others in the series," but the abyss "gets deeper with each additional determination." Maybe eventually we'll break through to China, or fall into a genderless (or gender-full) Wonderland. Or maybe we'll be filling up the abyss with images forever. Regardless, I think it's important to remember that we don't have to keep dropping the same images, the same kind of writing, down the hole, that if we can't crawl up and out, we can at least "go down," exploring more and more deeply the infinite possibilities of the category of "woman." At the beginning of this introduction, when I wrote that I was uncomfortable with posting signs and patrolling borders, I didn't clearly state what it is that we were cordoning off. Certainly it's not any one new image of "woman," as you'll see when you read the stories in this collection. If it is anything, maybe it's the abyss itself, which we've roped off not to keep the old "victims" out, but to give new ones a chance to fall in.

—Elisabeth Sheffield

Kristin Herbert

Kristin Herbert's poetry won an Academy of American Poets Prize and has appeared in journals including *Cream City Review*, *5AM*, *Kingfisher*, *Phoebe*, *Parting Gifts*, and *The Antioch Review*. Her fiction has appeared in *Central Park*. She's lived in Madison, Wisconsin; Pittsburgh; and currently she lives in Louisville, Kentucky, where she serves as director of marketing for Sarabande Books.

see also **Random**

A woman named Marilyn walked up to me in a bar in Indiana wearing toreador pants and high heels and something orange on top. "This is not my hair," she claimed, emphatic. "This is not me." Her eyes and hands pleaded to be believed. "I feel like an alien."

Ever since, when I think of bad hair, I think of Indiana. And because it seems like everything in Indiana is somehow made of or covered with cheese, orange on top like Marilyn, I think of my recent failure to buy cheese.

It was in the Strip district, an Italian marketplace in Pittsburgh. I was trying to buy Parmesan cheese. But there were two choices. That's the trouble with the United States: too many choices of everything. I read labels. I compare. I try to decide which is the better product, the better buy, and which is ultimately more important. Finally I leave without having purchased anything. I am no fool. I will not be a victim of deceptive packaging.

But because the market was not busy, and because the man behind the counter seemed knowledgeable and affable, I asked whether he noticed an appreciable difference between the domestic and imported versions of Parmesan cheese. The latter cost almost twice as much. He said "Night and Day."

Night and day. He sliced slivers of each and offered them to me on the blade of his knife. I sampled one and then the other. But which was which? And more important, which was better? Night or day.

My mind functions almost exactly like an index, only rather than being alphabetically arranged, the entries appear at random and are infinitely cross referenced. The logic seems arbitrary. It can be frustrating.

Arbitrary as in why cheese appears to be orange. Cheese, for the record, is not orange. It is the color of cream. So, of all the possible colors that could have been chosen for cheese—fuchsia, chartreuse, midnight blue—why orange? I can't answer that.

Orange has a peculiar mythology. Said to be impossible to rhyme, to incite confidence, and to signify insanity, orange warns of possible danger; beware. The things we take for granted, *see also* perception.

My basic beliefs are these: that *orange* rhymes perfectly with *door hinge*; and that confidence and insanity are ideas as abstract as color—extant only in the imagination.

But I'm still telling you about myself, not cheese and not beer, although that will be the next subheading. Remember, we're in the Midwest; or we were. The word *domestic* reminds me of a waitress at a restaurant in a small town in Wisconsin. When I inquired what the domestic beers were, I meant which of all possible domestic beers were available at the restaurant and/or how much they cost. The waitress told me that domestic beer was beer without alcohol. This is a bad thing to remember, as it happens to be untrue; but I find that the mere effort to forget anything makes it indelible. So whenever I think of Marilyn or hair, I have to remember that domestic beer has no alcohol. Which, as I have already told you, is not true.

Truth is elusive, inscrutable. Take, for example, the serpent eating its tail, a trite but vivid image and a symbol of infinity. I intuit that this transcends my understanding: a circle is comprised of an infinite number of points; a line is defined by two points; a plane is defined by three points. A circle, then, represents an infinity of lines in the same plane—effectively, tangents. I am reminded of spirographs. Somehow, this doesn't help.

Just as I think I'm about to etherize an idea and pin it down with words, it skitters away like a waterbug on the surface of a lake. I doubt the insect understands even the basic principles of its success. Rather, I suspect it skitters on instinct alone. Similarly, I left my own husband a year ago; I wish I could explain. But that is a tangent; I'm getting distracted. The insect teaches that superficiality is survival.

Quicksand, often thought to be a tropical deathtrap, is said to be similarly survivable for mammals: the trick is not to struggle. To do that, you have to believe that giving up will let you rise like cream, which is, even in the abstract, incredible. Faithless, doubtful, I sink every time I imagine it.

Saying cheese is supposed to make you smile. Personally, I'm averse to it. I resent being told what to do. It makes my throat close; I think I'm choking. Once I had to throw myself over a chair to save myself from being Heimlich maneuvered by the man across the table from me. *No thank you.* Appearances can be deceptive, but we hadn't exactly just met.

Picture this (point and shoot; the flash is automatic): I am as annoyed as I look, frowning and rolling my eyes, which, because of the flash, look pink or red as if I'm possessed. I am not possessed. I was merely trying to catch the waiter's attention to say *check please, I'd like to leave now.* All told, I consider myself lucky to have escaped without being stuffed, sprinkled, topped, or smothered with cheese.

But whether or not you smile, after being flash-photographed you'll think you see stars. These swimming optical glimmers are perceptual tricks. After-flash retinal burn is a hazard of illumination. But try to live with it. Something always obscures something else, relative to the observer. *Syzygy* is a better word for *eclipse*: earth, sun, and moon lined up in any order. For example: the moon, when blocking illumination, looks black; but don't look at it directly.

Here I am again, on a tangent: insects can not only animate the surface of water to suggest rain but also illuminate themselves to look like stars For instance: what appear as fireflies in Indiana after a hot, humid day, are merely spectral has-beens, like what we see as stars: stochastic and elusive. By the time we perceive light,

27

its source has expired or moved through the vacuumed void of dark.

Imagine: the epicenter of the universe on a pitch black night; the sky sharp with stars in endless configurations; farm fields stretched out like infinity. A singular evergreen stands in the middle ground. Fireflies dazzle the fields, cluster as if strung in the tree like so many miniature, white, electric lights, pulsing in synchrony, echoing the galaxy. I feel undeserving, blessed. Afterwards, the sense of loss is worse than never having loved at all.

Have you ever been in love? Believe it or not, I've been asked that. "Yes. No. Yes." I say, nodding my head to convey one, then the next, not respectively. I am embarrassed. I've done it again. I'm so unconvincing. I look as though I'm not paying attention to the question. But it is not so simple. *It depends*, I want to say, *on whether you mean did I think so at the time, from within the situation, or do I think so now, in retrospect. And what qualifies as love.* Et cetera. But that would not be appropriate. So I vacillate and lose credibility.

Memory is an unreliable witness, a slippery slope. For instance: Look at a pair of black spots on a piece of white paper. Concentrate. Focus. Now, quickly, look up at a blank, white wall. What you see is your memory of the two black spots. They are not really there, never were. So was I, was he, were we real?

Now back to the page: Try to recall, exactly—were those actually black spots or holes or vortices in the white space reflected on the surface of the page? Were they really a pair at all, or coincidentally separate? See what I mean?

I think that I might be losing my metaphysical grip. Recently I tested that hypothesis at a highway wayside. There was a machine that said TEST YOUR GRIP! It had an enormous chrome protrusion with huge finger indentations. For a quarter, you could squeeze the handle and the machine would rate you: Hercules, Burly, Strapping, Puny, Weak, or Frail. I put a quarter in and squeezed with all my might, with both hands. The people going past could see that I was cheating. I was Weak. I guess it served me right.

At least, that's what everyone standing around watching me thought. Imagine: all of them, in plaid and pastel and neon, thinking I was morally weak for having cheated. They might as well have pointed their fingers at me and sung, in shrill voices, repetitive songs full of words that rhyme with "cheater."

But how do I know what people think? I'm not an omniscient narrator. I'm a mere first person singular speck in the universe and unreliable at that, as you've probably already concluded. Here I am again, assuming, making a fool of myself.

But why stop now? Although profoundly personal, the question of whether or not one is religious is often a matter of bureaucratic inquiry. I've been asked my religion three times this year: joining a health club, seeking psychiatric treatment, and registering for a dating service. Each time I look the person in the chin and say "none."

It's invasive. I'm offended. So why do I feel guilty? Because I assume they have a religion that enables them to judge and condemn me. Never assume anything: it's a rule I try to live by. Assuming can be dangerous. For instance, as a result of my assumption, I want to grab a pencil, look them in the eyes, say *how much do you weigh? Tell me about your deepest fear; and what do you find sexy?*

The last time I had a religious experience, I was on a subway pulling into Grand Central Station. The conductor entered our car, opened his mouth, and out came an incredible, live performance of a weather report. He seemed omniscient: he knew what had been, what was, and what would be, world without end. His faith was unshakable. He knew, without doubt, that after the precipitation would be gradual clearing. He knew what time the sun would rise and set. By way of benediction, he wished us a nice day. We clapped. I embraced the man sitting next to me.

Perfect weather was among us. We all smiled at one another, head-on, imperfect strangers in New York City, in broad daylight

29

at 78 degrees Fahrenheit. The relative humidity was 65%. We practically passed the peace.

Anyway, where was I? On some highway in the middle of Pennsylvania, going away from one place and toward another; I don't recall the particulars. The point is, a bird fell from the sky. Coincidence? Perhaps, but only in the sense of convergence: when this connects to that as if at random, and meaning is refracted.

Only spinning wheels, a random death, and, afterwards, being sorry. Tangents radiate toward infinite resolutions.

You can probably understand now why I find myself profoundly confused at trying to connect experiences linearly.

I'm not trying to be difficult. For instance, I suppose that it's no accident that the bird fell from the sky precisely when and where it did. I suppose this, and yet I also suppose its opposite. I mean, I'm not suggesting there was a design to the collision either. Things happen. What next?

Based on abstract calculations and vectors, I estimate that the bird and my windshield impacted at more than 100 m.p.h.; that fast. What the bird was flying from, or toward is pure conjecture. I think this has something to do with leaving my husband.

I am crying. No, I am not crying, but it's as if I am. Put it this way: I should have cried. Imagine: cracked seed in a beak, the supple curve of neck attaching thorax to the loll of skull.

I am reminded of beheading chickens. Not that I've ever actually beheaded a chicken, but I picture the image they leave on the retina. the way they flap madly from their own severed heads, prove that even death can be contested—with gasped, panicked contortions; with last, carnal gestures; and with wings.

Consequence: what follows logically from action, as when one at last understands the vernacular, sees the forest as expressed by trees. The meaning of it flew at me, an augury so obvious it slapped, sudden as a handprint flushed with blood across the cheek.

I'm lying. The meaning of it didn't fly at me. But I wouldn't be crying, as I lifted the bird from between the blade of my windshield wiper and the glass, if it didn't mean something. Then again, I wasn't crying. Actually, it wasn't until I lifted it by the wings and laid it in the grass that I cried. Truth is, I've never even been slapped.

Happenstance is patterned like lattice. For instance: my need to intersect with flight and failure, the still warm bird in my hand.

Here I must admit, I killed it. Whether I want to claim innocence or say I did it on purpose, and whether I want to say I'm sorry or I'm glad is irrelevant. Who would believe me! I left him a year ago. I had to. I loved him. I am telling the truth; I am. I could say *trust me*, but why should you? I can't prove anything.

Everything is equally important. For instance: the turnips are getting pithy; I wish I could be indifferent. There's so much to consider. So although I don't understand why entropy drives the universe, who am I to argue? Does truth conform to music or does music bow to truth? It's hard to say. My sense of things unravels (*see also* entropy). Where to begin is what puzzles me, as is where to end. It comes down to chickens and eggs.

Though few women know it, we are born with our entire quotient of ova. Vessels of eggs. When we hit puberty, we begin to lose them, ovum by ovum. The significance of this cannot be underestimated or explained.

From menarche through menopause, a female is said to be "reproductively viable." She will be asked "When was your last period?" She will have to know when it began. If she does not know, precisely, she will be treated as if she's an idiot. I want to warn these girl babies, to tell them what to remember, what's important.

There are so many questions and so few acceptable answers. Medical situations make me especially uncomfortable.

"That's a difficult question," I will say.

"It's not supposed to be difficult," they will say, "just say *yes* or *no*."

31

But it's never that simple. For example, before a recent x-ray, I was asked whether there was any chance I could be pregnant. I said, "Yes. I am sexually active."

The radiologist, a woman, repeated the question. I repeated my answer, elaborating that unless I were mid-menstrual, I could not be sure and that since I was not, there was a chance I could be pregnant unless abstinent, which I was not.

Exasperated, she repeated the question. This time I assured her that if I were pregnant, I would abort so as to obviate her concern. "*Yes* or *no*," she said.

I tried to win her as a fellow woman (even our solidarity seems oxymoronic) by lamenting that until we are afforded a viable, 100% effective form of birth control, we will never know for sure, will we? She irradiated me.

It sounded like a giant photo flash. I felt like a moth in a candle flame; or I would have felt like a moth. The lead smock I was wearing made me feel more behemoth than moth. Even so, I felt almost epiphanic. I thought for a split second that I could read her mind. She was thinking *Gotcha*!

She could see right through me. *Touché*, I thought when it was over. I'm lucky to have any memory of this.

Similarly, Marilyn—her hair thin with the skin of her scalp showing right through the frizz. Her hair should not be the point: an incidental, tangential, superfluous detail. And hideous: orange. I did not *try* to remember this. But I could feel her pain. No. I could feel, through her, my own pain. So much so that the next day at breakfast, relating her story to someone I hardly knew, I was moved to tears. He said, "My, you are a fragile flower."

I want the perfect excuse; it would be so useful. Just today, for instance, at a fancy luncheon, I forgot the name of the dean of the university. In fact, I mistakenly referred to *him* as *her* and he overheard me. Then I claimed not yet to have met him, having just been introduced.

I couldn't explain. There was a sudden *hush* and everyone was looking at me. I could have melted like a piece of cheese in

Indiana, could have gone past the point of melting, could have denatured. Imagine: me, all oily and plasticy, oozing across the floor and everyone busily pretending not to notice.

Pretending not to notice is a popular social behavior. For example: "I have a giant blemish on my nose," you may say. "Oh, I hadn't noticed," seems to be the appropriate response. And although we understand the politics of politesse, we are, nevertheless, mollified.

The lies we tell ourselves. (Desire, *see also* Denial.) For instance: at the fancy luncheon, after introductions and against my will, a tomato landed on my breast. Anyone who admitted to noticing might have said I put it there. But I would not have done such a thing. It was a complete accident. A psychiatrist would say I am in denial of my desire to have the tomato on my breast. *But this would not do, to let desire land on my breast,* I would protest. (I'm nonchalant—kick desire under the table, pretend it never happened, deny it.) He says I am repressed, that I sublimated into my subconscious the wish for the tomato to land on my breast, and the pleasure of having it happen. *Were that the case, perhaps I would have dreamt it,* I rejoin. *Ah* (he crosses his legs), *why so categorically against medication?* Yikes; it's a perfect system.

My friend Kate once said, "You think too much." I said, "Kate, what do you suggest I do when I feel a thought coming on?"

She said, "Well, have you ever tried being like normal people?"

I have, in fact, spent my life trying to imagine what that means. To be normal. Trying to be.

Isn't being what you're doing when you're not trying?

My mother used to take me to the doctor for every possible deviation from perfection. She would ask him, "Is she normal?" He would say, "Yes, she is perfectly normal." But she would shift from one foot to the other looking worried until he would get out his charts of normalcy and plot me onto its official crisscrosses to show her that I was normal. Perfectly. Imagine my dismay upon realizing there were no such states as normalcy and perfection.

Not only was I not what I had been raised to believe I was, I was not *not* that either: the concept of absence in a vacuum times ten and then some = adolescence; it blows the mind.

I am still recovering. He did his job, though, be reassured; I am not a good example. I was, he could prove with his graphs, at a given point in time, just as I thought.

Now I don't know what to think. Is this existential angst? No. That's Angst, with a capital A: German fear too fancy to translate. (*See also*, Disorders, anxiety.) Psychiatry seems lazy to me. It's so reflexive: what do *you* think? In a recent interview for psychiatric services, I was asked whether I had irrational thoughts. *You decide*, I wanted to snap.

I answered that in order to answer that question, I would have had to speculate on what kinds of thoughts were not irrational, on what is normal. You see how I begin then, on the Möbius strip of infinite regress.

Perhaps the sky is falling, perhaps the bird bears a sign of land. Perhaps gravity, perhaps flight. Perhaps happenstance or fate. *I don't know; she just left*, he will say in my absence. What happened, they will ask. Why are you crying? It is not the question that is difficult, but the effort to answer. *This isn't me*, I will say. *This is not my hair.*

34

Bonnie Tawse

Bonnie Tawse has written a collection of short stories, *Lock and Load*. Her work has appeared in *Asylum Arts Annual*, *Sniper Logic* and *Doppelganger*. Originally from the Sierra Nevada region of Northern California, she currently resides in Chicago where she works with inner city children on urban garden projects.

The Big Lick

All of my life I've had this incredible salt craving. I must have inherited it from my mother. One Christmas, as a joke, my family gave me a salt lick. Like cows have. I put it in the corner of my room, right on the carpet. Everyone thought it was real funny, me having this salt lick in my room. Real funny until it started shrinking.

The two Asian ladies down at the DaShonne wig shop weren't taking me seriously at all. They were basically ignoring me, humming along to some Johnny Mathis song, shuffling in front of the towering wall of wigs. The shorter one stood on a ladder to get at the wigs up high with her bright pink feather duster. Her slip poked out from her brown polyester skirt, the kind that are scratchy. She made swift, precise flicks of her wrist, as if dusting Austrian crystal. The fat one went to the cash register and counted change. I was eyeing this black wig up on the third shelf. One hot little wig. But they wouldn't look at me. So I pulled out my fistful of cash thrusting it in the direction of the fat one at the cash register. "Look ladies," I said, "I'm *serious* about buying a wig." Then they gave me some service.
"You like this one?" She pulled down the one I was eyeing. She handed it down to me on its white Styrofoam head.
"Yeah, this is nice," I said.
"Real hair, that one. Nice style," she said perched on the ladder. She smelled salty. The other one came over and looked at me and then the wig.
"This one?" she asked. "This one so conventional for young girl."

"I like the tight curls," I said poking my finger through a jet black curl. I said to the fat one, "I think it's racy."

The wig set me back 150 bucks. But the shorter lady kept patting me on the hand and telling me I was worth it. Sure I am worth 150 dollar human hair jet black curly wig.

My wig fits perfect. It fits me like a glove. I put it on and I vacuum. And I tilt my head to the side just so. I do a vacuum cleaner commercial right there in the living room. I wash my roommate Glen's dirty dishes with my wig on, smiling out the window over the smell of old soy sauce and ginger. L.A. might be on fire but I keep my hands busy in the water. A fat, loud fly hovers over my wig, I flick my head to make sure it doesn't land in my curls. Glen made tofu chow mein for the model with the three syllable name and protruding collarbone two nights ago. I turn on the radio to find some groovy music, but all I can get is riot news, so I turn it off. The model had our bathroom dripping in fine lingerie. At least six pairs of cream-colored panties, two camisoles, one peach, one the color of swimming pool water, three black bras and four teddies, all of them the color of pearls. Everything by Perry Ellis, probably from Saks Fifth Avenue. She used up an entire bottle of Woolite. All of my underwear is either from K Mart or Mervyn's. But I have a new wig.

Glen left with the model for a shoot in New York. The bathroom looking like a pruned tree without the slinky goods hanging around. After I finish the dishes I dry my hands and touch my wig. The curls are tight, nice and tight. I go down to the bathroom and start running some water for a bath. I open the window so the mirror won't fog up right away, so I can look at me and my wig in the mirror. The more I'm liking my wig, the less I'm liking my nose. It's so round at the end, so *nice*. The Costa Ricans next door are listening to baseball again. Every day baseball and at night wailing Mexican love songs.

In front of the mirror with nothing but my blue Mervyn's panties and my wig on, I play with my eyebrows and zig-zag my finger across my face, drawing imaginary lines. I wait for the tub to fill. The Cubs are up by 1. Steam starts to rise and I can feel my wig loosen, so I turn off the water, pull the plug. I head down the hall. The only way I'm going to take a bath is with my wig on, but the curls can't get loose. So I put on some creamy dreamy orange lipstick and get dressed again.

We have nothing on our walls, not a single thing, just bare stucco. Glen likes things clean. Licking stucco is nothing like the salt lick. My wig's in my bag and I get on the bus heading to Sea World to pick up my paycheck. Sea World sucks. They make you wear these awful shocking blue polyester uniforms with a big, stupid Shamu emblazoned on the back. We're on something like our twelfth Shamu. The place reeks of death. And the dolphins drop like flies. Yesterday I saw two old guys trying to drag a dead dolphin out of the pool. They looked like they were about to croak too. And the tourists are such a pain in the ass. They get excited by anything.

Having quickly picked up my paycheck, which is a joke it's so small, I head back to Hillcrest walking proud with my wig in my purse. The manager in the Sea World office said, "You're a fine team player young lady." I've never even *seen* him before. Near the edge of the park I sit on a bench. A Styrofoam cup of coffee burns the skin on the inside of my knees. The skin turns red and I hike up my dress to watch. This is my lucky dress from Goodwill covered with horses. Girls on the field across the street practice soccer, their legs all brown and muscular. I'm trying to conquer pain so I leave the Styrofoam cup between my legs. The sun burns my scalp. I am really sick of how sunny it always is here. Everyday it's sunny. And the breakable little old ladies scooting around town with their heavy pink sweaters on, buttoned up to the collar, like it's cold here or something. Do people get cold when they get old? The old Mexican ladies who live up the block have got it right, baring their soft brown arms to the big stupid sun that is always there. An airplane goes by and the bench I'm on shakes. The air reeks for a moment of jet fuel and the sky above the soccer field ripples with the shriek of the engine. I flip off the plane.

39

Hopefully the pilot saw me. Very few of us who live near the airport ever get completely oblivious to the airplanes.

Trini, my friend from Sea World, is way into scarification. When I first met her, she was selling Shamu balloons and her arms were bare. Pretty pale arms with very dark arm hair. They're really a mess now, all slashed up. They make her wear long sleeves at Sea World. Our boss thinks she's suicidal. He doesn't get it at all. And she's very sanitary, never had an infection. She's coming over tonight with a fresh pack of razors. On the phone I told her I'd really like to do something with my nose—make it more distinct. Or maybe something coming from my eyebrow going across the bridge of my nose and ending on my opposite cheek. She said, "Are you sure?" And I said, "Trini, that's a stupid question." She doesn't know about my wig yet.

Sitting there running my finger along my face, making the imaginary trail of the razorblade from my eyebrow across the bridge of my nose onto my left cheek, this little black kid appears from behind a garbage dumpster. He throws a fat blue water balloon at me. Only he throws it way too soft, way too slow. But it does catch me off guard. It bounces off my knees, knocks my coffee into my lap and the balloon breaks at my feet. My crotch is soaked, my thighs on fire, my socks wet and heavy. I'm clutching the empty Styrofoam cup in my right hand and breaking into a sprint down the alley that runs behind 4th street. After about two blocks I'm gaining on him, screaming, "Hey, why'd you do that?" when I get hit on the back by another balloon, this time hard enough to knock me on my knees. My dress sticks to my back and I get up and brush the bits of pavement off my knees. The kid is gone. I never even saw the other one. The spot on my back stings. My dress sticks to me in all the wrong places, and I don't have a slip on. I'm wringing out the horses on my dress, chewing my bottom lip, tasting creamy dreamy orange lipstick. I'm wondering if this has anything to do with what's going on in L.A. when I realize I've left my purse sitting there on the bench. And my wig is in my purse.

If I run back in a panic I know my purse won't be there. So I walk back down the alley slow. Sucking in for breath and going slow I come out of the alley and I see the bench and my purse sitting on it. I rush up to it. I sink my hands into it. I pick it up and peer into it. My paycheck is there, my wallet, everything is in there except my wig. I swing my purse over my shoulder and pull at my dress and begin looking around. Panting, I check out the people around me. From far away everyone looks like they have my wig on. There's a man walking his dog over in the playground. He has something in his hand. I cross the street and rush up behind him. He turns and I see it is only an old brown ski cap in his hand.

"You got a problem?" he says as I stare at his hand.

"No," I say, and I add, "Nice dog." It barks at me and I run away.

Back on the sidewalk I begin searching in bushes along the street and the trash cans on the corners. This one old guy in a filthy three-piece suit is digging through the can on 6th and he stops when I approach. Then he continues, not saying a word, just pulling out bottles and cans and McDonalds wrappers. He pulls out an old National Geographic covered in coffee grounds and offers it to me but I say no thanks. As people pass I look up to see if anyone has my wig. All I can think is, I'll never vacuum again. Then I realize I'm out 150 bucks. I'm walking a little haphazardly, wondering why those kids threw the balloons at me when I bump right into someone's bony chest, and before I can even look up I can smell cologne, Drakkar Noir, and I look up and see it's my friend, Rafael. I can't even say hello or utter his name before he grabs my shoulders and clasps down on them hard.

"Raf," I say, "ease the grip. It hurts." He lets go and looks at my dress. I haven't entirely caught my breath since I started chasing the kid so I breathe real deep.

"Have you seen a wig lying around here?" I ask. "It's black, a curly black wig, real tight curls."

Rafael has curly black hair but his curls are loose, looser than

41

my wig. He has no shirt on, his shorts sit low on his hips.

"You wear a wig, since when?" he asks. He pulls at my dress. "What happened?"

"Since yesterday," I say keeping my eyes peeled on all the action going on behind him. The eucalyptus trees which line the street are swaying. A huge Corona truck pulls up in front of Hubbib Liquor and blocks the sun.

"No I haven't seen a wig, but you know your velvet painting, the one with Jesus on the cross?" he says chewing the skin around his pinky nail.

"Yeah, what about it?" I say as he spits little bits of skin at our feet.

"Well, I stole it the other night." He squints gravely. "You were passed out on the couch, I got it out of the closet. I sold it for twenty bucks. I'm real sorry, I needed the cash." He drops to his knees right there in front of me. His kneecaps make a smacking sound on the cement. He clasps his hands together and drops his head into his chest.

"Please, please forgive me," he howls.

"Rafael, it's no big deal, my parents gave that to me as a joke one Christmas," I pat him on the head and twirl one of his curls around my finger.

"I'll get it back for you," he says and tugs again at my dress. He is still on his knees gazing up at me. "What has happened to you? We must find this wig." A little old lady creaks past and smiles at me.

"Rafael," I hiss, "get up right now. People are staring." He gets up, his knees are red.

"I will find your wig and your Jesus painting," he says rubbing his knees.

"Bring some Bourbon over later, okay?" I say as he heads down the street and he nods back.

I look all afternoon until it gets dark. My dress is dry but stiff. I'm coming to grips with being out 150 bucks. I'm wondering if this is some sign, that I didn't deserve it or something. I slip into the library and head back to the map section. Nobody's in there. I lick the huge topographical map of Europe. I lick all of Italy right down to the tip of the boot and a few of the Greek islands. I leave the building quickly, lick my lips and apply some more creamy dreamy orange lipstick.

I get on the bus heading uptown. I sit at the front of the bus, in those seats for old people. Across the aisle there's an old guy with this sweet brown fedora on. He reads the *L.A. Times*. Leaning across the aisle I skim the front page.

Below the riot pictures is a headline, "PENNIES ALLEGEDLY USED TO KILL WOMAN." I am able to make out that two rolls of pennies were taped inside an elastic bandage and then held against this lady's windpipe, crushing it. The man keeps shuffling the paper and the bus jerks to stops and lurches forward again. It's all I can do to not fall right into the lap of this old guy. I hear Rafael's kneecaps hitting the sidewalk and try to imagine the sound of a crushing windpipe.

"That's some fucking imagination," I say peering into the front page. The man pulls the paper down to about his chin, which isn't much of a chin at all and says, "If you want to read the paper, go buy your own. And watch your mouth."

"Sure," I say. "No problem." And I lean back into my seat while the bus stops for the blind guy that always gets on at this stop. Just as we get going I add, "Nice hat," as he pulls the paper up.

"Thank you," he says shortly from behind the paper. The blind guy sits next to him and smiles at nobody in particular.

I get off a couple of blocks from my house. Trini should be coming over soon. Now I'm not sure if I'm ready to face her and her razors and all of her scars on her arms. I'm drawing the line from my eyebrow across the bridge of my nose when I see Gunner, my old surf coach sitting on my porch. I never go to the beach anymore, Sea World ruined it for me. He's rubbing his arm, right below his shoulder. I yell, "Gunnnerrr," down the block at him. He spits and scowls. He keeps rubbing his arm. So I approach slow.

43

"What's up with you? What's up with your arm?" I say sitting next to him.

"Where's your sweet wig?" he asks looking at my head.

"How do you know about my wig?" I ask.

"I saw you in it this morning, you were vacuuming. That's one sweet wig," he says.

"Someone fucking stole it," I say rubbing my knees which feel bruised. And right then he pulls up his t-shirt sleeve. I whistle low and slow. It's a tattoo. In the bad porch light I make out that it's a tattoo of the last supper, only the Looney Tunes characters are sitting in for the real guys. Bugs Bunny is Jesus, sitting there in the middle of the table. It's pretty big and the skin around it is all pale and puffy.

"That's some tattoo, Gunner," I say.

"Thanks, I waited 'til my old man died to get it," he says lighting a cigar. "L.A.'s going fucking beserk, man," he says between sucks on the cigar.

"Yeah, maybe something big's gonna blow," I say. And then I say, "Your Dad died?"

"Three years ago. But he would have killed me if I had got one when he was around, so I waited. And then I took a long time deciding on the design and, you know, where it should go, and then finding the right guy to do it." He offers me a cigar, I put it in my purse.

"Bummer about your wig," he says.

"It's no big deal, I'm just bummed 'cause these black kids threw water balloons at me today. That's how it all started."

"Hey they're just kids, you know, they didn't mean it," he says.

"Yeah, whatever," I say, rising up. "What are you waiting for?"

"I'm waiting for something to happen," he says just sitting there.

"Me too," I say groping for my keys in my purse.

"I hear Trini's gonna slice you up tonight, can I watch?" he asks snubbing out the cigar on the mailbox.

"Who told you?" I say opening the door.

He gets up, rubbing his arm some more, "Dave the Wave told me, he and Trini are screwing."

Glen must not be coming back for a couple of days. The place is empty. "Trini and Dave the Wave?" I shriek in exaggerated disbelief. "That's some fucking couple," I say.

There is a half gallon bottle of Jim Beam sitting right in the middle of the living room floor. I don't know how Raf gets in here, with the doors locked. There is a note underneath the bottle, it says:

> the wig is so close I can feel it,
> don't start without me.
> I'm bringing bandages.
>
>   RAF

Trini arrives wearing a nurse's uniform about three sizes too big for her. She has a nurse's cap with a huge red cross stitched on, and white hose and white nursey-looking shoes. Dave the Wave comes with her, his blonde stringy hair looking greener than usual, and he's obviously stoned. He's carrying her doctor's bag and wearing Ugg boots and smiling in a slow way. Gunner and Dave the Wave talk about the surf today and Gunner explains how he doesn't surf anymore, since he moved downtown, sold his board and bought a Harley. But the Harley got stolen a few weeks back so now he walks everywhere. Rafael shows up with a velvet Elvis and hangs it on the wall.

"Just until Glen gets back," he says, hammering a nail into the stucco. I wince as little flakes of the wall sprinkle onto the hardwood floor. We've never had a hole in the wall. I've got a craving hitting me hard. Gunner skips out to grab me some barbeque corn nuts and a grape popsicle. I start laughing at things that aren't even that funny because I'm starting to get a little

45

freaked out, looking at the razor lying on the white towel on the coffee table. Rafael takes boxes of new gauze out of his pockets. Trini rubs her arm and says, "You've got to be sure, this is permanent shit, this is for-fucking-ever." Raf and Dave the Wave nod behind her, pouring shots of the bourbon into Glen's hand-made sake cups. I belt another one back. Raf and Dave the Wave actually hate each other, Raf won him in a skate jam last year. Dave the Wave fell off the ramp and broke his collarbone. I got hit by an out-of-control board at that jam and got a bloody nose. But tonight they're being civil. The news is on with the sound off. CNN shows aerial shots of the worst parts of L.A.. And they keep playing the videotape of the beating over and over again.

"I wish they'd fucking quit showing that," says Rafael. He stands under Elvis with his arms crossed across his chest. "It's making me sick."

"We should have to watch it non-stop for twenty-four hours," Trini says. Dave the Wave lightly smacks her on the side of the head. Trini pushes him. "Cut it out," she says. I can't tell if she's playing or pissed. Gunner rushes in the door.

"You didn't start without me, did you?" He throws my goodies at me. I'm starting to feel sufficiently buzzed to get things rolling.

"Let's get this done," I say slamming my sake cup down on the table. It leaves a little dent in the grain of the wood.

"Yooohooo!" yells Gunner. Rafael looks concerned. He brings in a chair from the kitchen for me and sits down near my feet. Trini brings a towel and wraps it around my neck. Like they do when you get your hair cut. She was in cosmetology school for a couple months at the beginning of the year. And just like a hairstylist she stands over me, only holding a razor instead of scissors and she says, "How would you like it?"

"Come from above my eyebrow, go across the bridge of my nose and stop at the beginning of my right cheekbone," I say pulling my pointed index finger across my face.

Dave the Wave lets out a long whistle. Rafael giggles.

Gunner changes the station to cartoons and keeps an eye on both me and the TV.

Trini is swift in her strokes, like an artist. I flinch at the sting but then I feel so dizzy I can only feel the blood on my face, warm and cold at the same time. The last thing I see before I see the flash of the razor is that Rafael has gotten the Polaroid out of Glen's closet. I can hear him shooting away. And I hear Dave the Wave running to the bathroom. "What a puss," says Gunner. The blood trickles down my nose onto my lip and I lick and taste it. And it is salty. It tastes good. It has a calming effect.

Trini starts dabbing at me with her towel and I see the blood, it's splotched all over it. It is very, very red. No one says anything, no one asks me if I'm okay. I'm okay, but still, this gets me a little ticked.

"Don't look yet," Trini says, pressing the towel hard on my nose. "Raf, give me those butterfly bandages."

She rubs a circular motion on my back and she says, "Honey do you want some Beam?" I nod staring at the blackness of the towel, licking around my lips, and wonder what I'll tell my mother. And about Sea World. And how much better I'd feel if my wig were on my head. And the map of South America in the library and how good the Andes feel under my tongue. And how I'm gonna go to Nordstrom's tomorrow and buy as much lingerie as I can get my hands on.

Eurydice

Eurydice was born on Lesbos and grew up in Alexandria and Athens. At fourteen she ran off to Hollywood. Her novel, *f/32*, was published by FC2, and her numerous short pieces have appeared in many magazines and anthologies. She's currently a staff writer at *Spin* Magazine.

The Labyrinth

...before the silver cord is severed, or the golden bowl is broken; before the pitcher is shattered at the spring, or the wheel broken at the well, and the dust returns to the ground it came from, and the spirit returns to God. (Ecclesiastes 12:6-7)

8

What Pasiphae wrote all day and night was unimportant. She wrote not for posterity, but in order to keep herself busy and involved, but also detached and safe, in and under control; to keep from exploding. She never edited or experienced writer's block. She saw language as a tool no different from a suspension bridge. She wrote indiscriminately, out of a choking need, powered by nostalgia, to prove that time existed by naming it. She didn't care to distinguish the night from the blackness, the shadow from the eclipse, the scent of maple syrup on french toast from the steam of hot eggrolls, nor was she tempted to ever draw conclusions. She was the original writer: a failing record keeper. Pasiphae recorded the present, a realm that has no shape. She didn't aspire to make sense. She was simply and anonymously transcribing the refuse of history, writing against infinity.

Pasiphae never read what she wrote because she preferred to always find herself at the beginning of a text, in the proximity of that fleeting intimacy between her and a life she was unable to inhabit, like a Sisyphus climbing up a mirage. As a result, she had no idea how much time ever elapsed. She would lift her head every so often and notice with some alarm that her walls were overgrown with vines or her skin was turning blue. She knew that time and stories were seamless.

Sometimes, holding a pen, Pasiphae found that her hand refused to let it go even though she very much wanted to put it

49

down in order to caress a risen pale penis that reminded her of Jesus. But her right hand tightened its grip. The pen was the weight of an organ, a baby's heart or a puny liver, removed from a chest and nestled in the curve of her fist. She craved a shy boy's sperm trickling through her small fingers that instead grasped the ink-dripping pen with a visceral greed. Her other hand tried to intervene, but the diseased writing hand would imperceptibly and inevitably reattach itself to the pen it had just been made to release. What was striking was the naturalness of its gesture.

1

Back in the old country, where ample women carrying pitchers from the island well saw the sea leap into sky every sunset and so knew the world had an end, where Pasiphae had been weaned off her rebel mother instants after birth, everything (every wind, every abdomen, every shadow, every rifle, every grape) spewed forth stories; and these stories sustained the inhabitants during long periods of tyrannical oppression, when people had to dream up bonfires to keep warm, and heap the dead high to make shade, and live on fermented carob beans and crunchy grasshoppers. They whispered confidentially about a melodic well somewhere in the cliffs that hadn't run dry for three thousand years, and about gardens where watermelons grew big enough to sail in, and about winters when all manner of edible beasts were tossed like wriggling scapegoats from the seas. Thanks to these communal tales, the wardust didn't caulk their eyes, the conquerors' paeans didn't deafen them, the hunger didn't harden their souls, and almost all of them survived, and quite a few even fought back.

Pasiphae's own story might as well start at dusk during one such bleak period when her pregnant mother, Dido, belly bulging like an occupying tank, hands nimbly pressed beneath an empty clay pitcher, walked to the edge of town feeling her ripe anger balloon and wend its way through the blasted dirtroads, goading her to haul no longer water but the latest tyrants' blood; and to veer off her daily path and follow a parched whistling to the cliffs where she was met by a dozen solemn stormy men covered in scabs and odors, whose inner organs had long fled into famous battles, and who lived on the knowledge that beauty is ultimately preserved only in blood. Dido offered to join them in carving the new horizon. And so at the moment when other women were gathering their big black skirts and kneeling over the bucket to drink, or turning the squeaky crank against their wide hips, Pasiphae's mother smashed her pitcher against the inhospitable cliff and with a shard sliced her hand to mix her blood with her new warmates', then drank it and vowed on her unborn baby's soul not to bring water home again or perform any domestic chore but instead to cheat and whore and pillage until her country was led to freedom.

2

Pasiphae's father, Androgeus, spent his life looking for his phantom bride, Dido, whom he lost first to the peasant rebels, and later, more dramatically, to the Cretan sea. For the first four years after she'd vanished, he tried to find Dido or even recreate her in Pasiphae; but incest was a mighty obstacle. The more he struggled to mould Pasiphae in his beloved's image, the more he realized that if one looked too closely at anything, one risked coming face to face with the Devil.

"What did she look like when you were alone, Dad? Did she have a smile?" Pasiphae at the age of nine or ten would ask him as they cuddled under the night. She asked because she feared that her own memories were unfailingly fictitious, usurped from library books. "Your mother was an ogress. She wandered into this bed in pitch darkness smelling of cigar smoke," Androgeus would reply, squeaking his side of the mattress so nervously that Pasiphae imagined him rubbing himself in the manner of sunstricken cicadas. "She bled smoke from every pore as she lay her pearly canines against my neck. She was a biter. Every night she took another chunk out of my spine. I became afraid only when it hit me that sooner or later I'd run out of meat. But how

51

I loved being eaten! I rocked in this bed against the constant chopping and spilling of her seawash, my hulk full of seasick sperm, listening to her mindless slap-slap; 'Give me some of that good stuff,' she'd say, smacking her lips as she hauled me into an undeniable ocean. Every night I grew lighter, and I begged her to suck me up like water suckling at the leaky chineboards of a skiff. But she didn't have the time. One night the phone rang.[1] The world erased itself in a cataclysmic wave when I picked up the receiver. Someone said she'd slipped underwater, no traces, no sodden corpse."

3

Androgeus's father, Sarpedon—may the wave that embraced him turn to port wine—didn't want his son to be a sailor: "Stay away from the hauntress," he advised Androgeus, "she has no pity or faith. Worship her all you want, sing her praises, she'll stick to her cunning. Sooner or later she'll dig your grave, son, or she'll spit you out, a bag of useless bones. Sea or woman, the same bottomless trap, misery, a gap under our feet, can't be tamed," he chanted on during holidays, those rare seasons when he wasn't diving for treasures and sponges or running bootleg cargo on Libyan-flagged ships. Like most men on the island, grandfather Sarpedon was addicted to the ocean.

After he quit the sea at age 69, Sarpedon simply transferred his loyalty from one liquid element to another, and in the process he retained his seaman's phobia for narrow bathrooms, and so he kept a blue Tupperware bowl on the rough cement under his four-poster where he presumably peed in secret while the town slept. No one knew when and where he emptied it. He was widely known as a gifted drinker and, after disembarking, he made his living as a wine-consumer at weddings and festivals. He was paid to cajole the guests into the bacchanallic ecstasy and memorable brawls that guaranteed a feast's success, and this he did by challenging anyone to outdrink him, bottoms-up, telling nightlong

---

[1] *"The phone can ring at any moment, honey: such is its horror!"*

seafaring stories and generally setting a good example. A man who lived off his drinking couldn't logically contain so much liquid inside his gaunt body, and yet the townsmen who spied on him for nights on end never caught him in the act of emptying his bladder. In time he grew famous for holding his liquor. His belly gurgled from miles away, and many claimed that his swashing reserves of urine served to perpetuate his illusion of being at sea.

After her grandfather's example, at an early age Pasiphae began struggling to capture the inexorable currents of the sea inside her tiny bowels, and extend her insides to contain its might, and as a result she refused to pee. She bloated by day, and liked to voyage in her nightly wetted bed whose wooden bars rose like the skeleton of a skiff, to float on her slippery back and navigate through her whirlpooling desires as if they were pungent waves, forging a hydraulic destiny for herself, imagining her childish body to be the lubricated finger of God.

According to island lore, the Phoenician family descended from Thalassa—later known as Poseidon—and, naturally, every man in Pasiphae's genealogy had died at sea. Even old Sarpedon, who spent his final days at the wineshop sucking alternately on a rusty nargileh and a wine barrel sprocket, sighing and shaking his skinny head at fellow drunken sea veterans, breathed his last during the baptism of a fancy yacht that met a storm on her virginal route around the town's rocky harbour. Her owner, a moneyed returning expatriate, her crew and the saluting revellers, all drowned within a mile from shore with enough sweet red wine in their bellies to console those left grieving that the dead hadn't noticed the passage from inebriation into ocean and extinction.

Historically, the sea had been the Phoenicians' family mausoleum and also their collective treasury. Although the men, out of a deep-seated superstition that a reversal of fortune always loomed imminent upon the next wave, complained that the sea had no money, each one of them could have bought a fair-sized island with their profits if they hadn't invested it all back into the sea. Instead, the different generations competed over who would

53

build the biggest boat or become captain younger or carry riskier contraband freight. For their dry-land entertainment, they cruised the island's shipyards.

And young Pasiphae, who noticed the gap between the men's warnings against the sea and their lovestruck actions, could not solve the mystery, and imagined that God propelled their souls down into the off-shore waves like the wind pulls rocks off a cliff, out of sheer gamesmanship.

So long as her mother lived, everything Pasiphae saw—the leather-skinned sailors in loose white linen shirts, the wooden nautical curves, the long-tressed unmarried girls singing of salty men, and the echoing sea that rode over the pebbles foaming and chasing the heart of the earth as if to cool its flames—ignited her desires. Every morning she left her warm wetted bed and ran to the shore, where she tried her best to anger the water and feel its foam on her skin like the saliva of a rabid beast. Whenever she watched a liner lift anchor and leave the port lit-up and whistling, her ropes taut like ink lines, Pasiphae's heart nearly cracked under the weight of her envy. And when tragic news of ship-wrecks submerged the island in black, and every face she knew turned wrinkled and mute, and orphans wailed through the streets, Pasiphae wished that her own flesh had been this raven-ous sea.

And yet Pasiphae's father was the only Phoenician in memory immune to the call of the sea. Androgeus had forsaken water for the woman; the fluvial passion that overtook his ancestors for taming the wet consumed him when he saw Dido stroll down the cobbled harbour promenade, poised like a prow's maidenhead, eyes flashing like blades, nipples tight against the starched lace, her lustrous hair unleashed on invulnerable shoulders, and he ached to glue himself to her, to call himself her; to irreparably be her. The more he stalked her, with the patience of a tongue poised on the edge of a clitoris, the deeper he became convinced that the world could be reconstituted within her, and that God might have created the seas from Dido's body fluids. As he daily chased her, breathless like a marathon swimmer, Androgeus recognized that the magnet that had pulled his forebears to the sea now propelled him with iron desire toward the footsteps of this undulating woman.

"You can have her if you deny the water," Dido's father Rhadamanthys, the winemaker, argued. His son Glaukus had just drowned in a vat of honey and old Rhadamanthys was eager for male descendents. "I make enough wine each year for you to swim in, if that Phoenician blood kicks up." "But I'll be shamed if my wife's fortune feeds me," Androgeus protested. "That woman is a life's task. So long as I live, I'll bottle the wine and you the girl," Rhadamanthys ordered. "After that, you mind the children and stay away from the docks. Keep her harnessed, son. She has no psychology." "Thanks to Dido, the sea holds no secrets from me, don't you worry," Androgeus promised, "its timeless spell has been shattered like an old clay pitcher."

With that guarantee, they proceeded into the requisite bargaining, set the dowry, and a three-day wedding ceremony ensued where the wines flowed as if Poseidon himself had struck his trident into the rock. Being a present tense kind of woman, Dido knew that if it wasn't this man it would be another, so she stomped her foot and protested her acquiescence, impatient to at last be rid of her girlish hymen. As for Androgeus, he found his Elysian exit in the saturating vacuum of her vagina.

4

Perhaps what followed—the revolutionization of Dido— could be explained in part by old Rhadamanthys favorite speech, which he missed no opportunity, festive or mournful, to repeat to anyone present, and which Pasiphae had heard a few dozen times and so figured her mother must have heard at least a thousand. It went, with little variation: *"We are men, we; we're islanders! We've taken a crooked path like a badly captained ship, yes, but we're not garbage; and even if we are, we'll live on and grow powerful and glorious, like before. The ironwood—it stays ironwood, no matter if you axe it down. The lion is a lion even after you shave off his mane and chop off* his tail and pull out his nails and his teeth. It's nature —and it's how we're made!

Look to the East. There the sun rises, brilliant and never setting. Now look West: molten skies, falling shores, weighted by tears and spleen; water tears our land to shreds, eats at it, beats it pitilessly. But look the other way, toward Constantinople: weather of diamonds; seas of holy water. God's gaze falls on those parts. You sick? Swim there to be healed. Eyes blind or hurt? Rub in that water and you'll see new worlds. You're deaf? Drink it and you'll be hearing harmonies.

The first foreigner's stinky breath dried the roses of our unspoiled city; his slobbering kisses sucked away her sacred blood. Conquerors, too many and worthless to name, have since been running over us like centaurs in heat! They disembowel old men, molest pregnant women, lie in our rulers' beds, flatten our monuments and call themselves by our names. Ships come and go, carrying off our souls. All our hallowed symbols are looted and shipped to the barbarian West, to civilize it.

Only St. Sophia's altar didn't join that unholy procession; they tried to steal away the sacred marble slab that Justinian put in the heart of his temple over which so many victorious psalms were sung as our best men offered sacrifice, but it refused to be a slave within museum walls; the foreign ship gaped in half and the altar slid out into the Eastern Sea. So now when we sail in that direction, we smell the myrrh that rises from the seabottom and feel we're men, invincible! And as out of the chalice comes the Christian's salvation, our salvation will rise from that drowned altar; our rebirth will dawn when our altar crawls ashore. Then we'll claim back our wealth and our stories. We'll get back Constantine's sword and our temple's gates and the Wise Men's clock and our bronze horses. The West will be poor and humble again, and the Far East will not dare look at us with greed, and our city will again be the universe. Yes. Because we're men, we! Men and Islanders!"

5

For their first two years together Androgeus and Dido lived by their axes and their genitals, working the vineyards and their bodies. She was sixteen when they were joined by the town priest and pelleted by handfuls of sugared almonds and silver-leafed rice, and within the year she conceived. Work and love and no time. The arid soil hid their seeds from chickens and birds, heated and resurrected them until they took on creeping ferocious colors, shapes and smells. But by the time Androgeus had learned to plow, Dido had learned to leave no fingerprints, and by the time he could prune, she could hijack and ransom; during their first successful harvest she was practicing how to assemble and detonate explosives, and as soon as he adequately trained his palette to recognize premium vintages, he'd lost her to the revolution. From then on, Dido stayed under Androgeus' roof and name only as a cover up; but she offered him no fidelity, no privacy and no respite, for her life was not hers ever since she'd signed it over to the Resistance with her blood. In revolt, Dido had found release from the needs of individual self-expression; she did not have to choose; she only had to behave heroically. She lived in a vibrant streamlined world where good and evil were lucidly defined. And she liked the ceremonial urgency of adlibing history that enveloped whatever she did.

Everyone knew Dido was charmed, protected in her rebellion by some biased patron saint, because despite the risks she took still living in town instead of taking to the mountaintops, she had never been arrested, interrogated and forced to sign-and-recant or be executed. Because of this, her most important task was recruiting each successive generation willing to die for the cause, and, later, visiting them in jail with clothes, glasses, patriotic small talk and medicine, easing their last days as well as recording them for foreign relief organizations. She had sat countless times in military court as some close-shaven man in fatigues read the simple word DEATH, without emotion, after the names of bright-eyed boys and girls not old enough to vote if elections had been legal.

She was an inscrutable—and for the Resistance, irreplacable—woman. When deathrow inmates saw through the narrow grilled windows that led to the courtyard above a pair of modish cherry colored pumps with bows and slender heels, they knew Dido would be appearing any minute like a portrait through the square window on the metal cell door in her cherry colored pillbox hat, smiling. "I found you!" she'd say; "You're alive!" with never a worry in her gaze. No one knew exactly which generals or generals' chauffeurs she befriended and with what favors she paid them off. But somehow she managed to break no-visitor rules, to locate aquaintances in ministries whose signatures could save lives, to laugh charmingly as she argued the going price of a head on behalf of those whose families could afford it, and to whisper last-minute Resistance directives with her parting kiss through the bars, waving goodbye with a confident hand clad in a cherry colored lace glove.

Because of this, Pasiphae had grown to confuse her mother with the angel of death, and shivered with dilated eyes on the pitch-dark nights when Dido, ignoring the curfew, came home, and on her way to Androgeus' bed would stop by Pasiphae's open door to glimpse her daughter's shape over the wall-to-wall sacks of grenades perennially stored around Pasiphae's bed. Then Pasiphae would hold her breath, and her clenched mouth would taste full of the thick mud of sand and blood that composed the prison courtyard into which the sweaty feet of the condemned would sink every dawn, as they stood to be shot, calling out "Viva!" or "It's so silly that we're dying."

6

Soon after Dido vowed to resist, and after he'd taken Androgeus aside for a drunken man-to-man in which he told him, "Now you better be like that hairy-chested prophet Elijah, boy, who carried his oar on his back like a shovel and headed for the mountaintops where no one knew his name," old Rhadamanthys slipped on a landmine left over from the last war while experimenting with a homemade method of breeding drosophylla on crystallized honey, and so blew up his skull, bequeathing to his descendants thousands of mutant flies and a dozen barrels of excellent vinegar. By then the town was almost a barracks, the bitterly embattled locals had forgotten the fine nuances between old wine and new vinegar, and Androgeus wanted only to hide like the prophet Elijah.

So after Rhadamanthys' burial—pompous despite the meagre times because Dido's presence prevented the usual antiestablishment looting by the rebels, which made the funeral a rare safe social event for oppressors and oppressed alike—Androgeus sold off the vinegar and the land to an assistant prosecutor's clerk and took a job as the city's librarian. The family moved into a whitewashed house attached to the marble library near the harbour, which Dido quickly cluttered with muffled printing presses. Because of the insurmountable restlessness at home and in the streets, and since the war had closed down the schools, Pasiphae whiled her days in the library where she strolled in step with her frowning father, hands behind their backs, among the abandoned rows of books that sat buried on neatly numbered dim shelves in the festered labyrinthine corridors. Naturally, no one needed literature in times of pestilence.

Androgeus found solace in the hollow echoing library, as much as he could in anything, given that he felt shamed by his wife's illegal independence and that he also suffered from an astonishing thirst for her. In vain he fasted or ate pulped rotten hogfish, transcribed ascetic treatises onto pighide or alphabetized extinct volcanoes, for no labor and no attrition could release him from his ghastly yearning to slip once and for all inside the robust and lucid gorge of Dido's body.

By his side, little Pasiphae inevitably played with words instead of toys. Raised in a world where the greatest shame was to break down and talk, she cultivated her silence like a Zen garden and learned to use her writing hand in place of her vocal chords. She rewrote old myths and hoped that, like her namesake, when she came of age she'd also seduce a raging bull, white like God's semen.

Pasiphae masturbated for the first time when she was five, soaking in her mother's lionclawed bathtub, secretly reading a yellowed library copy of Shakespeare's *Anthony and Cleopatra*

59

propped against her waterlogged knees. She didn't quit when her wrist began to ache and her labia clammed up and the water turned stale and chilled; she imagined her bathtub as both barge and Cleopatra, and read the same passage over and over, *"The barge she sat in, like a burnish'd throne, burn'd on the water.... At the helm, a seeming mermaid steers. The silken tackle swell with the touches of those flower-soft hands. From the barge a strange invisible perfume hits the sense of the adjacent wharfs. The city cast her people out upon her;"*[2] she alternated the emphasis from syllable to syllable until she felt sure she'd written it herself, for her own gratification. Through this bare endeavor, she first perceived the three cardinal methods of attaining pleasure: usurp, imagine, come.

7

Even in the darkest times of civil oppression, Dido wore striped silk turbans and swung a flashy purse that impeccably matched her stiletto heels and bulged with inky terrorist leaflets. She had a small mouth, a milky body odour that could go provocatively sour, sumptuous dense hair, a bosom like Lolabrigida's and the thinnest of bones. When she met clandestinely with foreign activists to pass on encoded torture reports and the rolls of film that she carried like tampons in her vagina, she liked to clarify first that "On this island, we dress up." "The closer you live to death, the better you should dress," she calmly explained to them, jingling her gold bracelets triumphantly.

Dido was the kind of prodigal woman who could slaughter time and space by wearing a mini and standing in an oh-so tilt against a cypress in the sparsely planted park. She knew how to launch herself hard and precariously against the night and feel at home in the gutter under the blurry stars. Minoan labrys and Doric laws, Macedonian swords, Roman puke, Byzantine pomp, Saracen fleet, Venetian walls, Turkish mosques, German kings, Nazi tombs, U.S. bases, nuclear arms, shredded comrades, stark

---

[2] *"and Antony, enthron'd i' th' market place, did sit alone, whistling to th' air' which, but for vacancy, had gone to gaze on Cleopatra too. And made a gap in nature..."*

varying light on yellowfaced harborlining wallsharing houses with vineyards on the roofs—she contained it all.[3] She planted bombs in government offices and machinegunned naive ambassadors, shopped at elite boutiques with Middle Eastern oil money and danced the nights away breaking plates with the city fathers, she conspired under torn cots in batshit-strewn peasant shacks, she daily changed codenames and histories, and she felt it all pulsing in her loins like the ripening and rupturing of a mature graafian follicle. She knew nature would take care of everything else, unthaw the flowers, moisten the fruits, nudge the sun up gold, if only she kept resisting.

Life for Dido was a game with death: she liked to flaunt how narrowly and frequently she could escape it. Some said that Dido grew tired of winning and too curious about dying toward the end. So she was "killed" one dawn in a half-assed ambush at the harbour, on her way to attend the dawn's executions, decked out in royal purple. Her alleged attackers were an apologetic fumbling duo who wept publicly for the mishap and mourned her by sporting waist-length beards and widowers' black. They were tried but released either on insufficient evidence or because they were the army's paid peons. After all the conflicting theories had settled, the islanders agreed that Dido had fallen or been thrown into the harbour and her corpse probably lay lodged in a cracked rockbed where the island's lost history was silting up. Amateur spearmen and seasoned spongers hunted for her, and it was months before the city gave up searching for its Dido through the slickgray water, but her corpse was never found; and yet no one questioned her demise, convinced that Dido would not abandon her homeland and its Resistance of her own free will. She was

---

[3] *In her most captivating still (which Pasiphae took with her to exile), Dido stood smoking under a soft-focus light. A torrential town seemed to be crashing down towards her from above in static flood, and she stood impertubable amidst the shadowy currents of gutters and boulevards, staring into the chaos as if she had spawned it and as if contemplating vanishing into her vagina and leaving behind the world in darkness.*

Chick-Lit 2

thought of like a legendary shipwreck, a monument to the fickle-
ness of the Gods. And when the government changed a few years
later, little bronze statues of a windblown Dido were erected in
the island's schoolyards and squares.

Pasiphae was eight or nine when her mother drowned, or
disappeared. Because Dido had always been too big for mater-
nity, like a transplanted Amazon, Pasiphae now suspected that
Dido might have outgrown the local revolution and run off to
become a global myth. But she was bequeathed no farewell signs
or other tools to bridge herself to Dido's absence and to death, and
the shock of that suddenly missing center led Pasiphae to view her
little mortal body as an excremental impediment to her mind's
striving for translucency. Death taught her that she would never
feel comfortable in her flimsy body, because (or so long as) her
mind didn't feel capable of dying.

In response to all those unanswered tongue-tying questions,
Pasiphae vowed to fight reality to the end, to record her own death
step by step year after year and thus defeat it, to leave no
unquoted gaps. So she inadvertently became a cold-blooded
archivist and an avowed dysphemist. Following Dido's uncer-
emonious disappearance, no one ever saw Pasiphae free of pen
and paper.

In the meantime, to escape his drowned mate's saltant
succubus and the prosaic logistics of keeping house, Androgeus
moved into the public library, like a shattered pharaoh would
move house into a pyramid. Outside the august neoclassical
edifice people bred, slaved, sacrificed and died, but within the
high marble walls Pasiphae lived untempted. In her new home
she achieved impeccable control of her bladder, she wrote in the
bathtub, on the toilet, at dinner, even in her sleep, and she never
again ran ecstatically to the sea. And this is how Pasiphae fell into
writing at that vulnerable age when other children fall into dry
wells or unobstructed manholes or wolves' malodorous jaws, and
continued to fall unimpeded for years since texts are by their
nature bottomless...

0

As Pasiphae blossomed into puberty, Androgeus, half terrified of his own body's unspeakable excitement and half disappointed at his daughter's less than dropdead Didoan bloom—the cynosure of Pasiphae's voluptuousness being a beauty spot between her eyebrows, that according to legend had also graced Helen of Troy—climbed out of their bed one night and never returned. Pasiphae divined that he must have gone in search of her mother at the bottom of the sea, an assumption that the civic authorities shared and so underwrote the expense for a husband-and-wife iconic Christian burial over the man-eating harbour. As a civil war orphan, Pasiphae qualified for the army's coveted relocation-abroad programs, but as the sole informed inhabitant of the island's only public library she was kept at her father's position for almost two years, the time it took the city secretary of books to reach a consensus among bribed interested parties on the right man to fill the vacancy, making sure he had rightwing politics and—caught in the mistrustful paranoia of the times—that he even walked on the righthand side of the streets. A blood-drenched period of peace had just begun—orchestrated by the puppet-government as a betrayal of the guerrillas who were promised amnesty for turning in their weapons and were massacred as soon as they did—so the city had reason to expect a resurrection of its public functions, and was recklessly investing in flower beds, fountains, toilets and librarians.

During this acidifying time, while Pasiphae fanatically wrote and rarely ventured out of doors, news of Androgeus' adventures reached her through the library walls. It turned out he hadn't jumped to his death but joined a monastery of orthodox cenobites because of his painful urge to lash himself, live under the sign of the fish and think in symbols. He craved an unfenced elutriated life, divorced from past and future, with only a monk's knife under his belt; and because cenobites didn't tie the stone of silence around their necks as a noose, he exchanged his solitude for their brotherhood, eager to share a common audible quiet with celibate men who did everything—cook, plow, defecate, bargain, or hallucinate—in packs and extended their prayers like a dam between them and the world.

Monasteries were popular refuges in times of terror, and Androgeus became one of dozens forfeiting worldly pleasures for the safeties of God; as the ceasefire had turned to genocide, the persecuted rebels sought bodily salvation in the Church they had mocked. Androgeus had joined for two months when the island's octogenarian father superior expired under the political pressures and was succeeded by a hot-tempered reverend, strong as a bull, with a foot-long beard beating savagely in the slightest breeze and a fiery gaze beneath his joined black brows which some associated with Mephistopheles. He was the only man who could command the small army of ad hoc monks that had suddenly accumulated within the ancient limestone walls of the island's monasteries, for rumour had it that he'd lifted a wild horse a meter above the ground in one hand. He was a lover of wine inclined to toasting himself in unintelligible Byzantine at vespers, and his pyrotechnic crisp authority tortured poor Androgeus (now renamed brother Elijah) because it reminded him of the underground plots and corporeal instincts he was struggling to shed. But as every monk knew, the Devil was infinitely wise and wily, and Elijah nightly flagellated his scrawny flanks more passionately than ever as a result.

One festival day, when the monastery traditionally celebrated the nameday of St. John the Hungry with mulberry grappa and salted sardines on unleavened seaweed bread offered at the end of mass to the faithful, the secular crowd waited in vain for the gates to open in hardy welcome. At first they assumed the good fathers had overslept and feared waking them by ringing the ironcast bell, but eventually they did so and panicked when its ominous clanging failed to produce the abbot towering livid like Zeus before them. Their escalating anxiety turned them into a mob that sawed through the heavy gate to the handle inside, then kicked open every cell's door and, finding them all empty, one by one climbed trembling with pity and fear up to the father superior's quarters in the ramparts. There the carved door opened practically by itself and revealed, piled unceremoniously on the unmade bed, exhibiting grotesque signs of surprise and delusion, each still holding tightly to a long curved sword of the kind villagers used to skin pigs, four dead monks. When their eyes grew accustomed to the dark sight of massacred holiness, the festival-goers counted five more cassocked corpses lying face down on the blood-soaked wooden floor surrounding the unvanquished bed.

The village priest was summoned and the victims were buried in silent haste while church bells rang monotonously throughout the island and the police set out on a fearsome manhunt for the father superior and the missing Elijah. During the orgy of rumours that followed, it was said that the monastery, as satyrists would want it, had a bristling sex life. Housewives sighed profound moans as they conjectured in whose bedroom the virile father superior was presently hiding. Men argued that logically the tenth monk could only have been in bed with the abbot, and scholars mulled over the fine points of whether the abbot had been miraculously saved through the will of God or the Devil. The mystery was finally enlightened by a witness who came forward when the church, in shame, noting that ignorance justified licentious talk, and hoping that fact would prove more moral than fiction, announced a monetary reward to anyone who could shed light on the mushrooming scandal.

It was then that sister Dorothea, a nun-in-training who, dressed in black from head to toe, often mounted the steep hill from the village to sweep the church and do the monks' washing, admitted being in the abbot's bed during the ill-fated uprising. Her front-page picture in all the dailies sold more copies than the king's birthday photo, and showed that under the shapeless peasant's garb beamed a sumptuous girl whose great almond eyes shone with a bottomless lust. Newsreaders had no trouble imagining her pale feathery softness in which the father superior searched for his Maker, and the heavenly symphony played by her penetrated inner organs when he prayed on her like a calliope. People saved her picture to refer to in times of drought and remind themselves that a good sister's breasts could keep a man warm all winter and her thighs could keep him sane.

She needed the reward to pay rent, Dorothea told the police, puffing on unfiltered cigarettes. She told them she was eighteen and as innocent as nature itself and had made ends meet on her own since her father's disappearance with the Navy when the foreign allies had accidentally sunk the nation's fleet some years back; and she was saddled with a howling mother affected by the moon, who ate like an ox and had to be kept locked up. The only sane person she had left was her brother, who got her the job at the monastery where he was a monk. She mentioned that during the war she'd made her cigarettes out of dried donkey dung, and she had already been fornicating with her brother, brother Theodoros, when he brought her to the monastery, and there he started sharing her with the other monks in exchange for favors or extra food or work shifts or mere friendship, and they had all enjoyed this until the new abbot got wind of it and almost sent them to the bishop to be defrocked and shaven off; but when they offered him a clay jar of aged Samian wine, he spared them and took the wine and Dorothea under his protection. At first, for her safety, she slept in his closet when she had to spend a night at the monastery, but eventually he took her into his bed where she encountered the excesses of holiness. He told her he suffered from hole-riddled recurrent dreams and so he needed to indiscriminately fill up any hole he could, to atone for all the holes he'd opened. He also told her that sadly everyone he hated had long since died, and so he would enter her after Thursday mass and not pull out until the Friday matins, in order to console himself. At those times, the ancient monastery ramparts resounded with a low grunting sound like the rooting of a contumacious hog, and the breeze carried a rank odor as from a rotting hairy carcass. Gradually, Theodoros' head went dizzy with jealousy until he forfeited his vows and goaded his suffering brothers to slay the father superior like a boar, then bury his corpse in the underground tombs beneath the centuries' webbed pyramids of bygone monks' skeletons, and announce he had run away—a persuasive excuse since everyone knew the abbot to be a rootless man who hid his history under his fury and used his cassock like a mask. Dorothea was informed of the plot but had kept silent, as any victor's spoils would.

On the predetermined night, Dorothea's rapturous screams travelled to her vigilant brother through the open windows and, in his agony, Theodoros sped up the insurgent plan and signalled a few hours early for the monks' gruesome attack. Visible through the moonlit window drapes were Dorothea's white resplendent buttocks breaking like frothy waves into the father superior's pelvis; Theodoros was unable to silence his avenging footsteps and quiet his esurient panting, so as he kicked open the unlocked door and shouted: "You shouldn't have put the meat to sister, father!" leaping like a shadowy incubus onto the rickety bed, he was met by a bullet that drilled a hole in his forehead. Terrified, Dorothea tried to slip out of the battlefield by disengaging her impaled pussy from the superior hard-on, and as she did so she must have hurt the father who swore under his breath but kept on shooting without missing a beat, so that by the time she was fully off him and grabbing for a blood-sprinkled sheet to cover her nakedness, he had planted one echoing bullet per forehead and shouted "Ingrates!" exactly nine times. It was all over by one a.m. He was slapping Dorothea's cheeks to revive her, when a dishevelled Elijah rushed in, wearing a tattered nightdress, his flabby body bearing the countless red welts of his self-cleansing, and he stopped short of utterance as his sleepy eyes abruptly awoke to the community of butchered monks adorning the fatherly bed and to the pig-slaughtering knives they clasped and to their stupefied expressions. He suddenly felt the whole world collapsing irrevocably, or perhaps expanding irrevocably, and he later told the abbot he had at that moment experienced the life-changing shock the sailors aboard the Nina must have felt when their ship didn't fall off the end of the world but instead sailed straight into the Bahamas.

"A novices' mutiny. They didn't count on my rifle under my pillow. Get yourself some secular clothes, Dorothea, crunchy apple of contention, treacherous as the sea; you too, Brutus. We're going on a trip." Minutes later, led by the abbot's will and rifle, the three were riding their mules through tobacco-brown vineyards towards town, and arrived in time to take the morning boat to the capital. Dorothea had never sailed and enjoyed being wined and dined by the crew; as a result, she couldn't repeat the two men's conversations to the police except to say that Elijah, who had resumed being Androgeus, and who had always before looked oblivious as if reading a book that was invisible to all but him, now lightened up until the ex-abbot no longer had to threaten him. She was surprised by their intimacy, for she had seen neither of them so jovial before and couldn't fathom why they took so well to their new identities of outlaws. After disembarking, they philosophized as she strolled, mesmerized, in and out of the capital's glittering shops, and the abbot found them lodgings at a harbour hotel where he introduced her as his cousin. The lights of the taverns shone so tantalizingly while the men were shaving off their beards that she begged the abbot's permission to go out. He replied that she should now find a new unspoiled lover to protect her, as he couldn't enter her again after so much brotherly blood had been shed over her sex. When she had returned to the hotel that night, she'd found no trace of either man.

It took months for the secret police to admit defeat and the two defrocked monks' pictures to headline the posters of Wanted Men on public walls. Pasiphae, daughter of a dead rebel captain and an excommunicated criminal on the run, could not escape her legacy: she was now invited into every conspiracy. If she peeked out into the early lilac morning to retrieve the fresh goat milk, the old milkman would whisper to her about a clandestine meeting at the prehistoric palace ruins—"in the Queen's bedroom, can you find it?"—and the grocer would nod stealthily as she picked through his shrivelled potatoes, and scribble dates instead of prices on her bill. Suspicious customers wearing large gold dolphins around their necks returned the library books with handscribbled maps folded beneath the covers and translations of codified alphabets hidden in the bindings; and there was always one or another shifty-eyed and homeless-looking secret agent tailing her. It was out of this labyrinth of conflicting loyalties and riddles, in which she refused to choose sides ("die Wahl ist die Qual"—choice is torment—she had learned from her parents, who must have learned it from her country's conquerors), that her delayed government papers—issued before her father was resurrected as national enemy and thanks to the bureaucracy not yet retrieved—lifted her.

On the day her youth-transfer visa was granted, Pasiphae boarded a rickety bus to the island's airport that stood tumbled-down in a barren field fringed with faded oleanders blowing in the ochre dust, beyond which sprawled the rosy hump of the Bacchus mountains. The air was low and hot and heavy, as if with the breath of unnumbered generations of dead, and that was the last breath she took on her homeland. For the next eight hours, during her emancipatory international flight, Pasiphae felt like Remedios the Beauty ascending with the wash. If God had existed, Pasiphae later thought, she would have immaculately conceived in the air that day, flying to JFK.

In the chaotic airport at what was to Pasiphae the end of the world (America seemed at least metaphorically like an end in a world that had become endless), and while nervously scanning for her native hosts who had only been described to her as a blond Christian couple, Pasiphae was almost tripped by a colossal sailor with fiery eyes beneath joined black brows who enunciated in her mother tongue: "Your father has taken to sea, he is at peace, he wishes you a happy new life." The stranger spoke in such a monotone rush that it took Pasiphae several nights of replaying his memorized message in her head to fill out the words that had seemed full of holes and separate them back into their intended meaning. His chore fulfilled, the messenger had hastily shone on her the twisted smile of someone who did not know how to go about the business of smiling and would be much more at home in derision, and with two powerful strides he had parted the madding crowd and vanished into the waiting jaws of America.

Some years later, when she reached legal adulthood, Pasiphae received in the mail a copy of her father's will couched in legal jargon. She never responded to claim her inheritance of the family lands on a sunny island which was now democratic and prospering with tourists. The letter informed her that Androgeus had been lost at sea aboard a swordfishing skiff, two decades after having denied the ocean for a woman; and Pasiphae found relief in knowing that she, as the last Phoenician, had one over her co-humans: she already knew where she would breathe her last, and it wouldn't be dry.

8

Before man invented time, when aliens were not alien and stories roamed free, when soprano sirens consumed willing pirates and Alexander the Great was an immense mermaid who crushed to death those who mistook history for truth, when pleasure meant pain and all things contained their opposites as an ineffable matter of fact, Pasiphae could have been quiet and blissful. But then fiction got replaced by memory, and men hunted and women gathered, and the soul was invented, and all the good things became illegal; and soon enough, America was "discovered."

Yet even though America was a well-endowed insane asylum, it had one saving grace: it possessed no memory. So when Pasiphae was first told "No!" by her hosts, she didn't bend under the weight of meaning and tradition because in America words were lightweight. And because America didn't focus on a past but a future, Pasiphae did not have to mistake that "No!" for an inexhaustible voice echoing out of her own deepest core and internalize it; so she took it as a declaration of war.

She turned the language into her playground, and she played so intensely that it did not kill her. She appropriated the vocabulary of those ordering "No!," keeping the hunger and shedding the fear. The world went by, clicking its heels, watches, and cases, like an ocean passing through a needle, and all the while she shaped its names with her fingers.

And even when she found a little failing God stirring inside her, she didn't give up her quest for an apocalyptic vernacular. Even after she discovered that the puppeteer was everyone and everything around her, she didn't stop looking for a world that allowed the fullness of being human. And when she didn't find it, she made it up; and she gave it back to the world as a war cry.

1

to be continued

71

Jessica Treat

Jessica Treat is the author of a collection of stories, *A Robber in the House* (Coffee House Press). Her stories have appeared in various journals, among them: *Ms, American Literary Review, Black Warrior Review, Alaska Quarterly Review, Asylum Annual,* and in several anthologies, including *Word of Mouth* (Crossing Press). She is completing a second collection.

Honda

I liked the name. If ever I had a child I'd name him that. I figured it was the kind of name that would protect him. Why did I imagine a he? No reason. Just that Honda wasn't going to fit a girl very well. Sometimes I imagined I already had him. I'd sit in the park with all the young mothers and dads with their children and I'd see Honda playing in the sandbox. He was a good boy. He kept to himself, never bothered anyone. Of course the sand creations he made, castles with drawbridges and so forth, were so fantastic that the other children begged to play with him. Or at least help him. They would pile sand for him. For example. Or they'd be the ones to make the tiny patterned imprints on the castle, from twigs and leaves and so on. Honda didn't mind them helping. He would be so intent on his project that nothing else could really interfere with that. It could drive you a little crazy. When I called him to dinner, when it was dark and time to leave the park, he'd still be sitting there, piling on sand and fixing bridges. He acted like he didn't hear me.

I'd leave the park in frustration. It's easy to get mad when no one pays attention to you. It happened on one such day. I was thinking about the mothers and their spanking clean children, the little snacks they always carried for them. Seemed like they always thought of everything. How they fell into easy conversation with one another. About their children, of course. I got into my car, started up the engine. I noticed as I pulled out of the lot that the car had a different smell, a cigar smoke smell. I looked around as I drove. I could see work gloves on the passenger seat and some motorcycle magazines on the floor. None of these were things I kept in my car—so how did they get there? And the key chain—a tiny soccer ball of imitation leather—wasn't what I carried. I had a little red pocket knife, the kind with miniature scissors on it. The more I looked around the more I saw that this wasn't my car. It was blue, it was a 1982 Honda, but it was someone else's.

Of course I should have driven right back to the lot, parked the car and gotten into my own. Isn't that what you do when you realize you've gone home with someone else's raincoat? The sort of thing that happens a lot—at tea parties or restaurants. I kept on driving. I had some sort of block against turning around. Maybe because of how Honda ignored me in the park; I didn't want to be seen by all those young mothers again. Or maybe it was just inertia. Whatever it was, my foot was on the gas pedal, the gas gauge was at half-full and I was going straight ahead. Apart from the cigar smell, which was kind of homey when you got used to it, the car was actually cleaner than my own. I mean I did have a lot of junk and things in mine: dinners that were half-eaten, crumbled cookies, my broken umbrella and favorite green sweater and things. I noticed also that his upholstery wasn't torn like mine was. I really don't know how he kept it so neat. After all, it was a very old model. He actually had a blanket on the back seat to keep it cleaner. I checked it out through the rear view mirror. I thought I could see dog hair on it. So he had a dog. A doggy type of individual.

Where does one go in a car that isn't your own? It wasn't at all clear to me. So I kept on driving. It occurred to me that I could bring his car home for him. That would be a real favor since he was probably wondering where it had gone off to. I had only to find his address. I waited for a red light to pull out his registration. There it was: Michael Todd. Chestnut Hill Road. Such a pretty name for a road. I had never been there. It gave me a destination. I wasn't exactly sure how to find Chestnut Hill. I searched the side pockets for maps. I found maps of Canada and New Mexico but no local ones. Obviously this guy knew his way around. You had to give him credit for that. Or maybe it was his dog, with the nose of a pointer. Always pointing toward home. Or was that a weather vane? I didn't know. I had never been very good at directions. In fact, I was getting more and more lost by the second. At least I had gas. Half a tank could go pretty far. I didn't have money to buy more. If I ran out of gas, Mr. Todd was just going to have to find his car by the side of the road somewhere. A sad thought for the Mr. and his dog. But they were used to walking. That's what doggy-types did: walk all over the place. Come to think of it, he might not even miss his car, being so used to walking everywhere.

It was very pretty this time of year: early summer. The lilacs were starting to blossom. I rolled down the window some to get a whiff of them, to kind of trade cigar smell for lilacs. They were wholesome. The road was a pretty one. I passed old barns and neatly kept houses. It was the time of year you could see people out in their gardens. All winter long you never see anyone and then suddenly they're everywhere like ants out of their tunnels: digging and planting and mowing. A lot of work surely. But then, you get that nice flower smell. And lots of it. Or you get a clean piece of lettuce. Or a bright red radish. The possibilities are endless. Too bad I never took up gardening. With Honda there just wasn't enough time for it. It was one or the other. Maybe Mr. Todd had time though. In between motorcycles and dog walking, soccer and cigar smoking.

Chestnut Hill. The thing to do was to ask someone. One of those gardeners. I chose a lady with a wide brim. Her hair was white and her skin aged from the sun. Didn't she take a break in the winter? "Can you tell me how to get to Chestnut Hill?" I practiced my most polite on her. She squinted at me. "Let me see now... Go back to town, take the first right after the light, go up a hill, you'll see a sign for it, off to the left somewhere ..." I nodded like I knew exactly what she was talking about. Her eyes were very blue. Everything else seemed faded. I thanked her. "Your garden is beautiful," I told her. She seemed genuinely pleased. "I'd keep a garden if it weren't for my child," I added, "you get so busy, you know?" She nodded. "My children are all grown. I probably have more time than I know what to do with. But I enjoy it really..." I felt she was on the verge of telling me things she might regret later. "Bye, ma'am, and thank you."

Driving on a road you've already driven on isn't so much fun. Back to town. I had a bad feeling about it. I really should have kept going, looked at more and more pretty houses and hillsides, maybe even lakes and ponds. I don't know why I didn't just turn around. It was the fact that I'd been given direction, been told where to go. It was silly though, because why should I care about the Mr. and his dog? Why should I bother to return the Honda when it suited me very well, fit like a glove to my needs and personality? The faded blue upholstery, the slate blue dashboard, the gas gauge on its just-below half mark all felt very intimate, like the Honda and I had been designed for each other. I was snug inside. I tried the radio, but quickly turned it off; I didn't like the intrusion of loud radio voices. I wanted the hum of the engine: just Honda and me, taking our time.

I noticed him as I pulled into town. He was right behind me. I sometimes see them where they're not; I see bars on a car roof— ski racks and so forth—and immediately I slow down. I don't like to take chances. But there was no mistaking this one: a spanking white car with blue stripes and block letters: State Police. I felt confused. Should I continue straight or try to find that turn-off, the way to Chestnut Hill? My plan, which had never been a very clear one, was completely muddled now. I put on my turn signal. I was following the directions Mrs. Cornflower had given me; I was on my way, my best foot forward.

That's when the lights started flashing red to the accompaniment of high-pitched screeching. It was my worst migraine turned inside out, the flashing and screeching closing in on me, blood-shot eyes all around me. I was sweating profusely. There was nothing to do but pull over. I suppose there was the other option of a high speed chase, but no, I didn't feel like I had that option. I really didn't. I turned the engine off. I looked at myself in the mirror, straightened my hair. Was that Mr. Todd in the car with his dog? I thought it must be. I sat back in the Honda and waited. I felt calmer suddenly.

* * *

There is no need to discuss humiliation. The kind of interrogation the police can put you through. Accusing you of stealing someone else's car when it was an innocent mistake: the car was exactly the same as my own. And let's not forget that the owner had left his keys in it. Mr. Todd. But I'm not supposed to know his name. We were never introduced. Not by the policeman or by our own selves. It doesn't matter. I was already aware of him. Mr. Todd and his chocolate Labrador. Mr. Neat and Tidy with a dog who sheds hair faster than you can vacuum. It was an innocent mistake. Even the policeman had to come around to this. After all: there was my own car looking very similar, except for the rusty grooves and pockets, in the parking lot. (Once I'd found a mouse living in a rusted out hole, practically under the car. She'd made a little nest in there. Maybe she was pregnant and had some hairless pink babes to deliver. But after she saw me, she disappeared. I wasn't going to disturb her.)

It was a mistake. I knew enough to apologize profusely. How could I be so stupid? I even said this. More than once. I was obviously distracted. I was thinking about my son. I needed to get to the hospital to visit him. A congenital defect... (did I have to specify what it was? It seemed not). They nodded in sympathy, eventually.

Of course my own car was not driving so nicely. It was louder than his (the muffler) and the gas gauge was only a hair above empty, as it always was. This was not the fault of the car, of course, but of my own economic situation. Times were tough. It's not that I didn't have a job—I did—but let me just say, the pay and hours were slight. In the past I'd had jobs which called for creativity, more originality, like when I worked for the Card Lady. I did all sorts of wonderful things for her, down to helping her with the text and the punchlines. But some things aren't meant to continue. Her company got bigger; she moved. I sometimes wondered why she didn't offer to take me with her. A sort of relocation/transfer. I wouldn't have minded. She didn't ask me though. She had her own reasons, I'm sure.

It bothered me that now my car was known. It made me suspicious as I drove through town. Word was already circulating, I felt sure. The way people looked at me as they walked, or stopped pushing their baby carriages to stare, made me uneasy. I felt sure I had a record now, at least a verbal one, at the police station. It all seemed so unfair. It could make a person very angry really. I decided not to dwell on it.

But Chestnut Hill. There was really no way I could go through life without knowing where it was. The way to Chestnut Hill... It felt like a good song or the title of a novel. Let's just say, though, driving your own car isn't the same thrill. The landscape I'd marveled at earlier didn't look so special now. Because what did I care about neatly trimmed gardens and houses? Yet minutes ago they had looked precious, inviting even. I'd been happy, driving along in a car that fit me perfectly... Sometimes I just couldn't maintain my positive energy. I'd read all those books on positive thinking, I'd put in my time in that arena. Sure... whatever makes you happy. Isn't that the philosophy? The truth is, sometimes you just want to let loose some zoo animals to tromp on the petunias and munch on the roses. Besides, an elephant or hippopotamus could liven things up. You get bored looking at all that greenery. A hunk of gray isn't such a bad thing after all—I felt better just thinking about it.

I had every intention of going to Chestnut Hill. Who knows? Maybe the view from up there would be something to behold. Would make everything else worth it. But the whole idea started sitting heavy with me, like half-cooked bread in my stomach. The experience of being pulled over by the police, no matter how much I thought about baby mice and hippopotamuses, left me feeling sour. There was no way around it. I even tried to get my mind settled on Honda, he could usually cheer me up, with his dark hair and eyes, his intense child-like seriousness. But I'd put him in the hospital with a congenital defect. This also bothered me. That I'd resorted to such an extreme. Obviously I'd felt desperate. It would take time for me to recover my equilibrium. Driving wasn't going to do it.

I pulled off by the side of the road, parked my car and started walking. It was late afternoon, almost evening. The thing is in the summertime the days are so long you never know what to do with them. They stretch out before you, the sun still shining bright past five, six, seven in the evening. What do people do with so much sunniness? There were times I just wanted to crawl into bed, into a nice dark cave of stillness. Maybe that's why I found myself entering the woods.

Even the woods turn green in the summertime. It's the most amazing thing. This absolute push toward greenery. Never mind that it's a prickerbush, skunk cabbage or poison ivy, it's still green and shiny. I always wear long pants; I'm not going to risk any of those bushes or leaves touching me. I don't trust any of it. Like fiddleheads, those ferny things. I've heard people eat them. For breakfast. Imagine! Fry them up and serve them in restaurants. Someone told me about it. Or else I overheard it: "I'm just dying to eat those fiddleheads! I can't wait til they're in season." Imagine that: fiddlehead season. You'd think they were discussing violins. The truth is, everything has gotten mixed-up. People eat things for breakfast now I don't even know the names of. Astonishing things.

I sat down at the base of a tree. I leaned into it. It felt friendly. Maybe I could even fall asleep here, wake up to a forest-floor breakfast. The idea was intriguing. I closed my eyes. I felt the sun disappear.

Joshilyn Jackson

Joshilyn Jackson is a displaced Southerner whose plays have been produced in Atlanta and Chicago. Her fiction has appeared in *Calyx* and she is co-founder and managing editor of Big Girl Press. She lives in Chicago with her husband and several diseased cats.

SixLips

Sam loves tulips, he says, and she has seen pictures of tulip farms in books, So: POSSIBLE. And on the paper in neat rows it is simple.

On the right side is:
- She has a yard so big it is called land and not yard,
- There are green things growing all over it proving things can grow,
- Underneath the green things is dirt, a lot of it. loamy and spermy smelling, you can just look at this dirt and think nutrients,
- If you put seeds in dirt and then rain came or you bought a hose,
- The end.

The left side is blank.

On the paper on the right side is a garden and lot of money and expensive lilies and tulips and Chuffy no longer needed to pay the rent. But things start creeping onto the left side. And now the left side is this:

▼ The green growing things that were PROOF of what's POSSIBLE on the right side have to be pulled out and then when you get a section done and then go to do the next section the first section has them coming back smaller and yellower already with longer more resentful roots,

▼ There are things like climate and what grows where and storms and bugs and fertilizer and petal rot if you ever got petals, and you can't throw bacon grease out the back door without killing things,

▼ With all the yellow things smaller Walley can't creep around the yard and is in the house all the time getting thinner and paler, moaning under the sofa for a bush a bush one bush a bush, and the fat neighbor never catches a glimpse of him anymore to call about the scary man naked creeping in her yard, which means no one sees him ever and he may have ceased to exist except as a tongue on her cunt in the dark, or even that gone and then who is the tongue?

▼ If you look up from the dirt, Chuffy is waving all frantic from the closest window and if you wave back he only waves more and harder and gets excited and drools.

If only you didn't hate worms, if only there weren't so many boyfriends clotting up the place, and what is the point of being beautiful enough to change your name to Glynnis if all your white dresses fucking have sweat stains in the pits and your veils are muddy?

Then there is no room on the left side and the right side is this helpless half page sitting there trying tobe possible all cramped with left side letters pressing up against it.

Glynnis gets out a lot of sticky paper, the kind that is legal size but has gum all on the back that you can lick and lick and then stick it places. It is the paper left over from when Sam first moved in and he was all this perfect juice and goodness in an envelope of delicious fruity skin and Chuffy was all sweaty and damp with jealously stalking Sam in this hopeless bumbling way. If Sam got scratched or harmed she would die and so labeled everything that could possibly hurt him, labeled in big red letters DANGER THIS HOT THING BURNS and HARMFUL POISON and THIS MAN CHUFFY MAY LOOK LIKE A BUNCH OF NOODLES TIED TOGETHER BUT HE REALLY WANTS TO SLICE YOU INTO PIECES WITH THAT AXE —> RUN AWAY. But Walley got addicted to the sweet gum and slid around under and behind things lapping up at any paper he could reach with his unnaturally long prehensile tongue until the bottoms came loose and curled up over the warnings and Chuffy kept peeling his label off unless she snuck up and put it on his back and what good was that when the potentially dangerous pieces were in the front.

She gave up labeling because she couldn't sleep with Walley thumping around all night on a gum high and then Chuffy tripped while sneaking up behind Sam, busting his own head open on the flat of the axe. Chuffy bled all over her when she helped him up, ruining her dress, you can never get blood stains off white satin, but at least he was too scared to pick up the axe again.

Glynnis gets her list and puts each thing from the right side on its own sheet of sticky paper in a pile. Then each thing from the left side is a pile by the right side pile and the left side stays taller no matter how she stacks them. Order is not important. So forget order and go thing by thing. She passes each paper under the table to Walley and he licks it until she takes it away and sticks it on the right hand wall for right side things and the left hand wall for left side things. Very high up. She looks at the left wall for a long time and that doesn't help. And then she notices it's winter. She can forget the right wall and think about left wall things that can be fixed in winter. The yellow things in the yard are brown and maybe dead forever or at least for winter so she puts a yellow check over the yellow thing problem. When the left wall is covered with checks she can forget it exists and hang prints on it and have a garden. And then the boyfriend clot is a winter problem, she can organize her boyfriends if she gets enough colored chalk.

Chuffy is the clottiest, swamping her relentlessly with awful clotty love, so him first. She can trace his areas with ugly red chalk but then she doesn't want a lot of red chalk in the house so he will just have to stay in the bathroom. Always. She moves all his computers in there with one monitor and one keyboard. There are computers in the bathtub and one on the makeup table and one on the floor by the door and long cords under the door to connect to phone jacks and outlets, but the cords are smaller than Chuffy and go in one direction in an orderly way so they are in all respects an improvement. It's hard to stuff Chuffy in there with all the whining and clinging to the door frame with his too long fingers and clinging to her calf muscles with his too long damp toes but it gets done. She nails the door shut and writes in big chalk letters all red DO NOT OPEN EVER NOT EVER!!!!

She does Walley next because she might want him to get her off later and anyway he is easy. It is just a matter of drawing a yellow frame around everything a person could get under or behind and then little paths to the next thing to get under in darker yellow to indicate they are for nighttime or empty room use. In gold she makes a path from under her bed up and around the frame at the foot to the mattress ending where her cunt would be if she was lying on her back in the middle and said hey Walley come here.

She saves Sam for her especial last and it takes a long time because his paths get to be hopeful flower drawings from his rocker on the porch to his bed to her bed and each thing going to each other thing instead of in a single loop because he might want to sometime go to the fridge without going to the window, the table, the bed, the sofa, first. The paths take up more and more floor space and they are wide with flowers and ribbons and crossing each other until they are like carpet and not a path but it makes Sam happy. Sam's feet going all over smears the chalk and the flowers get very romantic and fuzzy looking and ground in to the floor forever so Sam can never leave her. She puts a big red check on the boyfriends page and then it is still winter.

Go to the library, is what Sam says about the other left side papers when Glynnis is finished crying into the dirt and has admitted she can never make enough mud loose enough to drown herself in poetically, just enough to muck up the beadwork on another white dress. If it was Walley she could say, Oh the library that's so fucking getting back to nature isn't it ISN'T IT. Or if it was Chuffy she could just spit. But it is Sam and the rest of the winter is about sitting in the library learning mostly that books about gardening are boring and then looking at some more pictures of tulip farms which turn out to be all in fucking Holland and that might be the problem.

And it's too cold to be still shitting in the yard but then it's good fertilizer and anyway they already tried going to the bathroom and you can't. You have to take all the nails out and then you have to kick Chuffy into unconsciousness or else he comes bounding out all happy to see you and by the time you do all that you don't have to shit anymore until you nail the door back and then suddenly you do again. Glynnis can hear Chuffy tappy-tapping on keys all night and the grind of the modem and when his check comes she has to slide it under the door and he always tries to bargain his way into a supper date before he will sign it over to her and slide it back. And it keeps her up. Tap Tap.

Then he discovers a new noise to make. It is pounding. She hates it. Wet smacky flesh, pound pound. And she can't figure it out until after Sam has fucked her and staggered off and Walley has crept up to get her off and then her cunt feels like a swollen mass full of sperm and whatever crumbly things Walley was eating and she walks naked in the dark to hike her ass up on the kitchen sink and spray herself off with the nozzle thing and then on the way back barefoot naked in the dark she steps on it, flopped out underneath the door. It makes a stain the cat likes to sniff and sniff until she wants to stab the cat but spring is coming so she stabs the yard instead.

This turns out to be brilliant. Because if you stab deep enough and then stab around in a square you can stab out a piece of yard with roots in it and underneath is more dirt. Clean pretty fresh new dirt. Virginal. Pale. Shy,

She learns it is better to not stab in squares but first to just stab in a line about a foot long and then a few side stabs and then you have a tab of yard that can be pushed until it folds over on itself and then push more until it is a roll tearing itself out with root rippy noises, SATISFYING. Then you push and tear until it is a huge roll at one end of the yard and a clean strip of the new unused dirt behind it. She has to put long pieces of butcher paper over each new strip because seeds will come on little parachutes if you don't, bad desperate seeds on a mission. She can now put several big checks on the left wall and she is ready to plant things. Sam wants to know what the library said to plant and all she knows is not tulips.

It takes a long time to get to the seed store because Sam wants to LEAVE THE HOUSE and DRIVE HER THERE and he has to drive slowly with her in front of him drawing the path in chalk and he won't let her draw flowers because the engine wants to overheat but she changes colors a lot using only the pretty pretty ones and draws on quick leaves and curlies so it is at least a vine. She buys a bag of seeds, a big bag, fifty pounds, and asks if it will make flowers and the seed man says it will. They do flower, he says. They get groceries while they are out, enough for a long time, things in boxes that become food if you put milk in them and powder that becomes milk if you put water in it and canned things and then flat things that can be slid under the bathroom door for Chuffy. Most flat things are bready, like crackers and frozen pancakes, and even though she looks for a little while there are not any flat vegetables so Chuffy will have to keep on getting scurvy and she hopes that the rest of his teeth drop out before she is forced to pry open the bathroom door and smash them out with a hammer to make his grin less annoyingly gappy when she looks up and sees him waving and the good thing is that the bathroom has only one window so she doesn't have to see him always waving but even when she is in the side yard or the front he is still waving she just knows it.

Going home is faster because they can just follow the vine back which means she gets to sit in the front with Sam and rest her head on his shoulder and people driving past them think, look at her with her perfect boyfriend wow she loves him, but then Sam's arm is going to sleep he says so she sits up and maybe now the people think they are married. Married Married Married.

At home the rolls of bad used land have congealed into a single high hump and you can't see where the rolls end so her plan for orderly rows based on the rolls is fucked. It's better this way, now the whole yard is a single piece and she can let the hose go in the middle whipping around like a mud snake and she can take whole handfuls of seed and toss them about and then dance on them barefoot grinding them into mud with her white dress getting soaked and transparent and clingy and her veil whipping around. She looks wild and virgin sexy and free and full of nature with Sam watching. He comes into the yard and fucks her, her muddy feet in the air and her blusher modestly covering her face, her skirts pushed up into a white froth around them until Chuffy starts throwing himself against the bathroom window and screaming rhythmically in the wrong rhythm to get Sam's timing off and finally Sam gives up and goes to bathe in the hose. She has to go inside and stick her bottom half under the dresser for Walley and gets mud on some of the flower paths and scrubbing up the mud erases them and then she feels bad about getting off when Sam didn't but it was a good day mostly.

When the things start to grow it is not in little pushing brave points of green all saucy like kitten tails but in curls. That keep reaching towards each other tangling until they are a huge high mass of piled vine. Messy looking and not like Holland.

But Walley is ecstatic. He can go down the hole under the desk to the crawl space under the house and creep directly into the mass of green. He can slither around the whole yard. The plates of food she leaves on the floor start getting pulled under things again and being pushed back licked clean. He fills out and sometimes you can see his plush bottom lurching up pale and full as he dives around. The vine is scratchy and he is rashy and doesn't care that's how happy he is. Then the flowers come.

THE BEAUTIFUL FLOWERS. They are big and milky white and full and hangy down and there are thousands of them shining and weighing down the vine with their pollen and there is no petal rot NONE and the left wall is a mass of checks and Glynnis has the flowers in her hair and in her bed for rolling around on and in vases and bowls and in strings across the mantle and just when it is time to harvest them and sell them to pretty brides they start turning relentlessly into zucchini. There is no stopping them. You can only stop them if you pick the flowers really really fast and then they die immediately upon being packed into boxes to sell in town. And they can turn into zucchini much faster than you can pick them all.

The zucchini are rotting. She can't even come after fucking Sam because of the smell. Happy Walley reeks of rot. She could pick them but what could you do with thousands of zucchini? She could pickle them and can them and turn them into jam, but things like canning and making squash jam involve gaining a lot of weight until you have big motherly breasts and changing your name to something homey like Margaret or Bettina and a Margaret couldn't be in love with Sam, she would have to love a butcher or the fat neighbor.

And the smell of boiling down zucchini would make her want to kill herself, she just knows it, and if you are a fat Margaret you can't take poison and die on the white bed in your bridal gown, you have to die in some lumpy awful bungled way like sticking your head in an electric oven until you starve. So let it rot.

She does take a few and put them against the bottom crack of the bathroom door and push until some juice squirts up the door and the rest mushes under it for Chuffy who says he needs it mushed anyway to gum it up, and who says his eyeballs are loose from the scurvy and if his eyes pop out he can't type into his computer and use his modem to send away whatever he builds there, so who would pay rent?

There is nothing to do but wait until the vines die and sag down and then she stabs underneath their roots and pushes them in a roll next to the first roll but deeper down so they look like two giant soddy stair steps. And wait through winter. The next spring she forgets to cover the rows with butcher paper and the whole yard is dandelions before she even plants. She rolls that away and the next year something awful comes, a lot of tiny awful leggy somethings that might be weevils. Then after that she plants pansies which don't even bloom for two years so fuck them, she rolls them away and then later she hits rock and nothing grows on it and she rolls that away to find fire and lava that burn up the seeds and she rolls that away and there is more dirt but nothing can see the sun so she rolls away and rolls away until the humps of soil are stairs all the way down and through to where you can stand upside down. She is in China, just as far away from where the tulips grow, where rice grows in sticky mud and has no blooms only kernels for throwing, but maybe now she can leave Chuffy to starve away still loving and waving in the bathroom, keep Walley safe inside the upsidedown bell of her huge white skirt, and it will be her and Sam finally getting married head over heels.

Rachel Salazar

. **Rachel Salazar** is the author of the novel *Spectator*. Her fiction has appeared in various periodicals and anthologies. She was born in Paris, spent many years in New York City, and now lives in Albany, California

Paradise

One block from the parkway fronting the river, the two streets slant to form an intersection. This triangle encloses a small park, also triangular, fenced with iron, an entrance at the vertex of each angle, some Lombardy poplars, vertical branches casting little shade over the benches beneath. A girl drinks from a plastic cup; a man passes a bottle to another man. In the park's center, an obelisk rises from a granite base, some blurred lines of spray paint on one side.

South of the triangle a brick building is being cleaned, a section from the fifth story to the second draped in yellow and blue plastic sheeting that flaps and billows like a sail. A helmeted workman standing on the fire escape vibrates as he holds a sandblaster against the facade. The half-open door of an adjoining building reveals a short man in loose white clothing and a box-shaped hat. His hands and face are dusted with flour, and he smokes a cigarette.

Frank carries his briefcase, which bangs against his knees, and walks diagonally across the cobblestoned street. Head down, he passes through one of the park entrances. He turns, glances at the girl, pauses briefly, looks away, then up. As he scans the block, variously cast-iron and brick buildings, his eye stops at a round window on the top floor—he counts, the fifth—an oeil de boeuf, the white frame contrasting with the surrounding brick. A harvest motif—a festoon of leaves and fruit—encircles it, the wreath's serpentine ribbons crowning the frame, mullions separating four panes of glass. The window opens, then closes. From below, he hears the slam, forthright, abrupt, like the crack of a whip,

a branch snapping under the weight of snow, a car backfiring...
He looks up again, this time in surprise.

"That window up there—that's mine..."

Looking down at the face beside him, the upper part obscured by shadow, he could not remember what he could not see at that moment, for the features were still too new, and he was not yet accustomed to them. He took her gloved hand and squeezed it, for he mistrusted his own voice, which might betray his excitement by its boyish pleading, cause her to change her mind, to realize her superior position, her strength, to decide to play, tease, withhold. As he stroked the smooth leather, the seams ridged by stitches, he determined the shape of her hand beneath. He pressed it to his cheek, then pulled off the glove, which he crumpled and stuffed into his coat pocket, thinking that he must remember to give it back—or perhaps contrive to keep it as a souvenir of what was about to happen.

What had first struck him about her was her androgeny and the impression that she was not much interested in men. He clenched the glove he had pocketed, staring at the domino of shadow. Moving her head slightly into the range of the street light, she met his eyes, then began to draw her hand away from him but slowly, so that it did not seem as though she were shrinking from him.

Curiously inert, he felt nothing as he caressed the bare skin, her hand scored by criss-crossing lines, no spark of passion, neither attraction nor aversion, but a knowledge of the potentiality of motion, like caressing the fender of a parked car.

He had not noticed her immediately when he entered the room, and he forgot her name as soon as he heard it—not because it wasn't memorable—but because of a tic: an involuntary forgetting or assigning the wrong name as the introduction is made. This had inserted a kind of unexpected tension into a predictable dinner party, for he had to remain alert, hoping that he would hear her name repeated. This need for watchfulness on his part endowed her with a somewhat mysterious aspect that she would not have possessed for him otherwise, as he waited in suspense for a second address.

What remarkable hair! A bleached-white crewcut. The light behind her, a bright nimbus around her head, glistening like the pelt of some pale Arctic cat. Her fair skin was lightly freckled—like grains of sand on a white sheet or cafe au lait spattered on a napkin—over pretty, deadpan features. Her melancholy eyes—unmoving, ends downturned—made Frank feel both compassion and curiosity. Although she spoke little and then in a monotone, what affect she seemed to have was located in her smile. For him, the evening had gained purpose.

Could it have been another window? But there are no other round windows on this block. Frank examines the row of buildings, his eyes running from one rectangular frame to the next, some arched, mullions forming different patterns, some with four, some with six panes of glass. No, he remembers clearly the oeil de boeuf, a faceted iris that included from its vantage the park, two intersecting streets, the cast-iron and brick facades opposite, the silhouettes of water towers, a narrow rift giving on a view of the river, dark that evening but now a blue reflection of the summer sky.

He stands still for a few minutes, then walks slowly across the empty street The sun is still in the east; the shadow cast behind him buckles over the cobblestones.

Standing before the building's entrance, Frank cannot make out the number painted on the glass transom. He examines the French doors, two large panes like those to an old-fashioned shop but reinforced with wire mesh forming one-inch diamonds, rendering it opaque. Three doorbells have been installed to the right of the door; from them a tangle of wires passes over the top of the frame. He tries to read the name taped alongside the words Fifth

Floor typed on a piece of paper, but it is partially obliterated: one letter, perhaps two, missing at the beginning, then *ar*...another letter missing, followed by *in*. He puts his finger to the bell but exerts no pressure; instead, he tries the handle, pulling the door open, noticing, as he enters, a pile of envelopes on the floor before the slot in the door. He picks up a handful, riffles quickly through them, reading the names. Some are addressed to Gardiner, and there is a blue air mail envelope with no return address for M. Dupree. The stamps are French; the postmark is from Paris.

Hearing footsteps on the stairs, Frank carefully replaces the letters onto the pile. A tall dark man, who could be from anywhere—Greece, Ethiopia, Mexico—appears, swinging a branch painted orange.

The man, although he says nothing, seems to scrutinize Frank, who, feeling as if an explanation is being requested, blurts out, "Dujardin?"

"Top floor." The man steps over the pile of mail as he pushes the door open.

The walls of the entranceway are painted from the floor to about four feet above with shiny cobalt blue enamel, the rest, matte white, as though to delineate a kind of cosmology by color, a blue-white hierarchy. Frank runs his hand over the surface, which has a grainy texture as though sand or pebbles had been mixed into the paint. The floor is set with green-streaked linoleum.

As the woman began to climb the stairs, he followed, a step behind. Her face tilting toward him, she raised each leg slowly, tension in the denim thighs as the boots lifted off the floor. Her hands, mostly hidden by her long sleeves, clenched, gripping cuffs, seemed to lead the swagger of her black leather jacket, a repetition of the sullen defiance in her face, disappearing into the darkness, as though she were ascending to something dreadful or at least distasteful. Or was it ill-concealed contempt at his apparent anticipation? Had he been grinning like an idiot? Clapping his hand over his mouth, he recognized the drawn muscles of a smile, the expression of a kind of hysteria he felt might erupt as laughter—like premature ejaculation—but which decorum relegated to a slight unhinging of the jaw.

On the first landing, an arched window faces the park. The two men below seem in the midst of an argument, their voices rising in bursts of exclamation and expletive. The girl is no longer there although the plastic cup remains on the bench. Hours past dawn, the sunlight, like a dissolving cloud, retains a pink cast. A gust of wind sends a tremor through the poplar leaves, a shudder passing from one tree to the next.

Frank sets his briefcase upon a stack of bundled newspapers piled under the window, rests his elbows upon it, chin pressed into clasped knuckles, as he stares out the glass. A Victorian-style chaise lounge has been placed vertically in the corner: an empty niche. It is upholstered in a salmon-colored velvet whose nap is worn from the cushions, armrests/ headrest. A strip of metallic short-fringed braid hangs slackly, ripped away from its tacks. Molded like twisted cord, the neck of a bronze standing lamp grows like a stalk out of a lotus-shaped base, the motif changing to the imbricate head of a hooded cobra, a bulb screwed into the socket held between its open jaws.

The woman continued to climb upward but faster, glancing over her shoulder at Frank, as though in mockery, daring him to keep pace with her. As she disappeared at the top of the fourth landing, he felt as if she were fleeing, escaping him, trying to reach her door before he did, so she could slam it in his face, having tempted him only to deny him, as if all were a prelude to humiliation. Or perhaps she too was impatient, dashing up the stairs in a high pitch of excitement—this gladiator of love—to gird

herself with contraception's light armor, ready to leap into the
arena where the victor might end supine or crouched on fists and
knees, teeth grinding pebbles, biting one's own knuckles, screaming, dust on tongue—in eyes—groaning while the vanquished
adversary labored, panting, anxious, knowing that another task
lay before him, as the Greeks before the gates of Troy knew that
in conquest lay death—*la petite mort*!—

Was she a kind of siren leading him aground to be dashed
against rocks or some Circe of bestial enchantments? Would she
roll him, rob, initial, gag, humiliate, flagellate, whip; or pierce
nipples, foreskin...penetrate him...The dark figure before him
lengthened—was magnified, maximized by its relative position,
expanding his perception of this tiny white ermine—this mink—
minx!—this quiet, vulnerable, tremulous girl, a *juene fille*, her
fragility hardening into a carapace of black denim and leather, her
probably mousy hair peroxided into radiance, the pedestrian face
painted to express startled wonder! A woman need not be anything—she must simply look like something: a strapping Amazon;
a terrorist; a tiaraed princess; a comandante fatigued in motley
khaki, machete under her arm—a sexual assassin—death in the
saddle! a man's sex withering upon the altar of Venus!—

Cold air rushed over Frank's stomach, a shiver elevating the
dark column of hairs trailing from navel to pubes. The woman was
in the bathroom, the door was open. He could hear water running.

Anyone could have lived in this space—although more
plausibly a man than a woman. What Spartan bareness—no,
barrenness!—stoic rejection of all comfort and decoration—utter
functionalism in her denial of ease: no cozy cushions, easy chairs,
sofas; only a hard-looking chaise lounge to sit on; no paintings,
drawings, prints; neither objets d'art nor trouvés; no bric-a-brac,
no kitsch...This asceticism seemed masculine; or perhaps it
corresponded to the woman's bleached, etiolate androgeny, the
abandonment of any quality that might characterize woman's

vanity and frivolity. To be neutral—possibly neuter—is of course a quality in itself, rather than the absence she probably strove for.

The loft was large—about four thousand square feet, he estimated—the walls not pure white but smooth and well painted; the floors stripped but not varnished, as though the gloss of polyurethane would be too brilliant, too showy, as though no part should call attention to itself as distinct from the whole: modesty and self effacement in every detail.

He catalogued the absent feminine: no florid black-hearted tulips, fresh-faced daisies, cheery geraniums in clay pots; no exclusively female equipment in the bathroom—cosmetic jars and bottles, contraceptive and menstrual paraphernalia; no shriveled stockings over the edge of the bathtub or carelessly cast-off slips and panties tossed over the back of a chair. There were, surprisingly, no chairs at all. Could the woman have hidden all ordinary objects out of sight before going out, to establish the rigor of her life to anyone she might bring home?

Standing in the bathroom doorway, he watched her. Undressed, her body was unquestionably female once released from the ambiguity of jeans, sweater, boots. Pale stretch marks, raised like a row of scars, ridged her hips. As though self conscious, she pulled in her slightly protruding belly, sighing as she averted her eyes.

A great fatigue suddenly overtook him, yet, for some reason, he did not want to leave the expectant emptiness of the place, which seemed to long for activity... He was curious about the woman—not only as a lover but for other reasons: to know her in the way that only intimacy makes possible. He contemplated narratives of childhood, family... He knew almost nothing about her...What was the texture of her life? Why this bloodlessness? He longed to know this small white creature—to hear her voice again—low, quiet, the words clear, discrete—even if she didn't say anything interesting...

"Do you live here alone?" He was certain that she did.

She shook her head.

Although he was naked and had drunk a lot during dinner, his usual inhibitions remained: he did not feel aroused. Was he being foolish? Was it too late to change the seemingly inevitable course of the evening? What degree or kind of pleasure could this fey young woman bring him?

He considered carefully, clearly, with detachment, that he was probably being unwise, careless, reckless, impulsive—but why not? He had not allowed himself this kind of adventure for a long while, had reined in desire—denied it.

Looking at the woman, he thought that he had seen her before...at other parties, in the neighborhood, in the streets where he often walked...details of the pale freckled face glimpsed (lowered fringe of eyelashes beneath purple-veined eyelids, the glistening large incisors); the approaching boyish figure—a guessing game!—stirring his curiosity, soon satisfied as she came near—a girl!—her face was already familiar to him. But tonight why had he been charmed by her, followed her, bothered with her at all?...the forgotten name to be retrieved...

As though recalling habitual modesty, the woman put her hands over childish breasts—now a knowing Eve—lowered her eyes.

He hesitated a moment. He could still leave... His clothes were by the bed...

Catching sight of his reflection in the mirror above the sink, he was saddened by his own face. Experience had settled around the eyes: the deep vertical line between them veering from left to right; loose skin above, drooping over eyelids; a creased fan at each corner. Womanlessness and childlessness, conditions assured by solitude, the loss of the irretrievable...

Pardon, old fathers...

Blinking blue eyes, moving her lips, the woman slipped past him. Her body, still thin, suggested maturity: thighs spreading and buttocks faintly pocked; lowering breasts; heaviness of the upper arms and fleshiness of the smooth back... He followed her.

She lay on a single mattress on the floor, made up like a bed and placed within an alcove that separated the kitchen from the large unfurnished space before the windows. As he sat down beside her, he smelled her perfume, which seemed to hover above...the scent of intimacy. With one arm behind her, the woman supported her white spike-hairdo head. She did not move.

Frank was disappointed. She appeared to be pretending sleep, to have no interest in him. Apparently, she was not overcome by desire, passion, admiration, or even a sense of opportunity. He reached for her round, speckled shoulder.

Sitting up, opposite Frank on the mattress, the woman picked up a black brassiere from the pile of clothes on the floor, held it up, put it on, hooked the back. The puckered lace cups resembled some furred insect...twin tarantulas...

His finger slipping under her strap, he touched her lower back very lightly.

"What are you doing?" She spoke quietly, without inflection.

He didn't answer because he didn't know whether he really wanted to leave or stay... Should he let the adventure just happen? Yet he could not set aside all considerations or his own hesitancy.

She picked up her sweater as though she meant to continue dressing. Her teeth glinted in the dark.

The white sheets and pillowcase were reflected in the window, their pale geometry contrasting with the dark quilt. The woman in profile, her back arched, clasped her hands in her lap, the brassiere strap a Mondrian strip. Frank, supported on one elbow, the muscles of his trunk delineated and smooth as a Roman breastplate, saw his other hand poised in the reflection, fingers stretched out as though to span her circumference. The dark vacancies of eyes, nostrils, open mouth, navel, like holes punched into a surface...

"Your waist is so small...like a young girl's..."

Although she shrugged, perhaps attempting to show indifference to or disapproval of flattery, she seemed pleased. Probably, she had heard variations on this observation before, had come to expect it, would be surprised—even disappointed—were it to go unnoticed...

Without passion—or even its simulation—she rewarded him with a long, ironic look that very slowly passed over his body, pausing at his lips, before she met his eyes and seemed finally to acknowledge the inevitable conclusion to this evening. Her certainty somehow repelled him, arousing contrariety, a desire to deny this capitulation of which she seemed so confident. Dawdling, he could dress, then bend down, kiss her in the most casual way and then leave...a humbling reversal...

Yet already a kind of mild excitement was building within him—like a drink that first warms the face, spreading its heat down the throat, then torching the entire body. A pulse in his ears signaled his impending loss of self-possession...

Reaching forward, he stroked her, his fingers moving up her leg, hesitating at the hip, avoiding her pubes—a dark smudge— attentive to the abdomen, the small hard nipples—she cried out—he lost the rhythm of the caress, tried to continue as though he had not but could not fall into it again. Impatient with himself, he withdrew his hand.

"Why did you stop? You have such nice hands—"

He sighed. Everyone says the same things. Disappointment intruded upon his excitement: the repetition of events, the similarities between people, what they said—everything and everyone like something or someone else—uncommonness uncommon, the encounter unfolding into a recognizable pattern and, therefore, becoming only a reenactment of other adventures...

"Say something that I've never heard before."

She laughed. "You must have heard it all! Everything! How can you expect originality?"

Rising, he faced her from the other side of the mattress: her hair was silhouetted against the light—a full moon in the night sky, a dandelion in a field, a black cat's golden eye... As he reached for her, she appeared not to notice, ignoring him or pretending to. The white sheets fell in angled folds about her thin legs as she stood up.

Casually, he took her hand, interlocking his fingers with hers. "Sit down...next to me." He pulled her down beside him on the mattress.

They stared at each other. Glancing from his face to his shoulder, she touched his forearm, tracing the raised veins.

"Men always..." Her voice trailed off.

"Why are we talking?" He said it teasingly, lightheartedly, putting his hand over her mouth, her eyes terrified above his fingers, as though suddenly she were seized by mortal fear.

With one arm under the young woman's neck, the other over her breasts, Frank was clasping her from behind, his body curled commalike around hers. The discomfort he felt was twofold: he never liked sleeping close to a woman, preferring distance between them. More disturbing, this position reminded him of the deception of such chance acts of love—this close embrace, as though they were inseparable, a kind of physical cliché...wanton truth lurking somewhere behind the curtains, under the bed .

A breeze blew through the partially raised window, the winter-night air, although icy, carried a smell of decay from the air shaft. The sheets were crumpled but still stiff...The smell of love—excretions, perfume—was merely evidence of satiety. Probably nothing more or nothing less, but that's a lot, isn't it, he thought. Conjuring the sleeping woman's face, which was pressed into the pillow, he pictured her vulnerability: the stupidity of the gaping mouth, a dreamer's fluttering eyelids, the complacency of a woman who has just made love, smug after climax...

This woman had allowed herself to be taken in ways that women rarely do. She could not be as young as he had first thought: she had led him through a maze of intimacies, keeping the lead throughout—while his heartbeat accelerated, veins everywhere throbbing, deafening excitement muffling all sound!

She had asked him to crouch forward on his knees, her instructions annoying as though he were unimaginative or too inexperienced to know the mechanics of pleasure. This posture gave him the sensation of complete exposure—nothing left hidden or secret or closed, as though all the body's openings were extended to their utmost limits. In no way abandoned, the woman seemed to be gauging the effect of this disclosure, an indifferent spectator. "You don't like it?" she had asked.

Her left arm suddenly relaxed, as though she had entered another phase of sleep, fallen deep into its pit. Lifting her limp fingers, he placed them on her own thigh in a kind of reflexive caress. As he raised his head, cheek resting upon her shoulder, he saw the face he had imagined—but the eyes were open, rolled up, only the whites showing in insensible sleep. Her left hand dropped inertly, then seemed purposefully to settle between her thighs, as though in defense, protective.

Rolling over, Frank felt safer, buttocks unexposed. On his back, a sheet covering him, arms folded across this chest, he stared upward.

The high ceiling seemed impossibly distant, as though the mattress were at the bottom of a deep ravine or, like in a fever dream, as though it were receding from his vision. The trompe d'oeil patterns in the pressed-tin ceiling shifted like a kaleidoscope—ellipses turning to four-petaled flowers to concave diamonds to circles, then back to ovals. At first the designs seemed oriented vertically, then horizontally, then diagonally. He closed his eyes, opened them abruptly—circles—probably the dominant scheme...

* * *

Go back. They're both in the apartment. He's by the window. She's in the bathroom. He never went back to that apartment. He never repeated her name. He never said it aloud. He never called her on the telephone. He avoided that street, the park in the triangle. He didn't want to run into her.

But he kept the story, refined it, dramatized certain things, remembered the apartment in a certain way, forgot the name, pretended he had never known it... She became something else: nameless, faceless, her attributes reduced to hair, freckles, sometimes teeth; the body preserved slightly better, no longer young or fresh, not really alluring; he goes through motions, some things happen—climax, that small satisfaction, what we live for, where we live...

The story never fails to arouse—all the right elements—anonymity! androgeny! blond Venus! black leather! emptiness! boots! indifference! fear...

Was the loft really empty? Could a man have lived there more plausibly than a woman? *Spartan bareness? Stoic rejection? Utter functionalism?* Words...just words...There was a sofa...the same one he saw in the stairwell...not really a couch but a chaise lounge, salmon-colored velvet trimmed with metallic braid...She must have left it there when she moved...not many objects...but a few: a painting above the couch...vague...black tape around the edges or was it framed with old-fashioned gesso molding, chipped gold paint or tarnished leaf?...the image on the canvas impossible to recall. There were tall bookcases crammed with books. He refused to be curious about them, resisted the impulse to look at their titles...he did not want to know what she read...

The androgeny was his own idea—an ideal—but why? Is a woman who looks like a boy more attractive than one who looks like a woman? All kinds of explanations, the most satisfactory the androgeny of adolescence: a longing for youth, not boys...

The loft couldn't have been so large—four thousand square feet? Again, he has exaggerated the proportions, made it vast—it must have been half that size. The larger space a more exalted frame for the woman within ...

Were there really no plants, no flowers? He can't picture any...What about feminine equipment?... He didn't look into the bathroom cabinet...There was a toothbrush on the sink, perhaps two—a neatly rolled-up toothpaste tube, dental floss, a man's razor—one with a disposable cartridge...but the soap...scented, difficult to describe... He had washed his hands twice, sniffed his palms, enjoying the smell...

Stretch marks, protruding belly...sagging breasts—all signs of motherhood that he did not recognize, chalked up to age instead...yet she was lovely...Why has he made her less so? To explain his own reticence, his own coldness? She, the woman, since not perfect, failed to provide proper stimulation: his response to her imperfections...This story is about mastery...but who is mastered in the end?

Was he really curious about her life, her childhood? Didn't he purposely avoid such knowledge? She must not become a friend...must remain a flawed body under a platinum halo—the hair causes excitement, the body a kind of leveler— Can't lose your head over her, she isn't that great! The enchantress becomes bestial: a mink, long, white serpentine, furry, elusive, hard to get, hard to pin down, hardhearted—a minx—

He longed to hear her voice again...even if she didn't say anything interesting...

The voice, not the words: a kind of surgical operation: the sound extracted from the words... She couldn't say anything interesting, because he wasn't listening. To talk with her would have made her something else to him—from minx to woman...

Do you live here alone... She shook her head.

An important question, the answer ambiguous: no or yes?

Whether a man lived there might have been important to him; the story preserves her gesture but does not go any further. Whom did she live with? Man, woman, child? A lanky nine-year-old girl: a taffy-haired, brown-eyed tomboy asleep in a loft bed somewhere; or maybe not asleep, maybe straining to hear. In the story, they're alone. He thought they were alone.

His usual inhibitions remained... He did not feel aroused...

Blame implied here. Her fault, not attractive or skilled enough—in fact, she was not active: his memory of her hesitancy a projection of his own? This is complicated. He was there but felt nothing, his movements those of habit...you don't leave a bedroom until you've done all you can do—penetrated every opening, taken complete possession... Despite his progress—his mere presence—the outcome not at all settled, rejection is possible, even probable; his coolness a kind of preparation for disappointment...

He had reined in desire—denied it even...

This part is true. A man of long solitudes...Why had he left this in? A touch of verisimilitude? He can change her more easily than himself. A whole history of self-denial, self-pity... A man who denies himself love can better deny it to others... A kind of fairness: no more than I have allowed myself... Restraint needed to resist a tendency to riot; rigid control simple: no choices: all is forbidden ...

Her face was already familiar to him...

More justification. He can't sleep with a stranger; thus, she must be a friend...but why didn't he recognize her later?...The identity a whole: no part can change without altering the entire self... Her face belongs to the hair, unrecognizable without it...

He could still leave...

105

Elizabeth Graver

Elizabeth Graver's short story collection, *Have You Seen Me?* (Ecco 1993), was awarded the 1991 Drue Heinz Literature Prize. Her stories have been anthologized in *Best American Short Stories 1991* and in the 1996 and 1994 editions of *Prize Stories: The O. Henry Awards*. Her fiction, poetry and essays have appeared in such journals as *Antaeus, Ploughshares, Glimmer Train, Boulevard* and *Story*. She teaches writing at Boston College and lives in Somerville, Massachusetts.

Mammals

It began with a walk in the woods with a friend I taught school with—a walk in the woods, no common thing these days. The trees were dark, barky, gleaming; the ground was covered with slick, brown leaves. We were walking, murmuring about this and that, touching trees as we passed by. Suddenly an animal leapt into my friend's arms, wriggled joyfully, licked her face. He was some sort of burrowing creature, too big to be a gopher, more the size of a small dog. His fur was bristly and dark, his snout long. The tip of his penis showed, pink and tender as a tongue; I saw it for an instant as he squirmed. I thought he looked something like a boar or a pig, a muskrat or a groundhog, although of these animals, the only one I had ever seen in the flesh was a pig. I backed up a step, ready to flee, but my friend was laughing deep in her belly, throwing her head back and squirming as the animal kissed her, until she half lost her balance on the slick leaves.

Then she thrust the animal out to me—a wriggling, twisting shape. I backed up, afraid. What if he bit me? What if he had rabies? But then he was upon me, overwhelming me with his sheer enthusiasm. He was at once ugly and immensely affectionate; even in his ugliness, he carried the beauty of any living thing. As he pressed his back to my face, I saw the intricate way his fur met his skin, each shaft tunneling into a silver-gray scalp. I felt, beneath my hands, the flexibility of his spinal column. I caught, in a glimpse, the glassy, dark brown curve of his eye. Then, as if a window had opened in his flesh, I saw through the walls of the animal's thick heart muscle to the ventricle, with its cells of muscle, tissue, nerve and blood—and inside those, to the membranes, ribosomes, proteins, chromosomes; and inside those, to where protons and neutrons, quarks and leptons spun. I saw the animal's skull with its carved eye sockets; his toenails like mica or plastic; his ribcage like a person's or a ship's.

We left that day reminded we were animals. We were quiet on the way out of the woods, our breath shallow and rhythmic. On my hands I felt the grease of his fur. That night I slept with his musky smell in all my creases, as if I had just mated with him on the forest floor.

We went back for walks when we had time, telling no one. Each time, we tussled with the animal or found others like him brushing past our legs, or nipping the cuffs of our pants, or leaping headfirst into our arms. Sometimes we walked for hours and saw nothing but each other. Other times we could not keep the animals away; they prodded at our fingers with their snouts as if we were hiding treats. Nothing, we said, opening our hands, showing our blank palms. They licked at our palms—the salt there, the sweat, maybe some sugar left from a pastry. Their tongues were rough and tickling, and soon we were on the forest floor and they were wrestling with us, licking the whorls of our ears, making small grunting noises, so close we could smell the dirt smell of their breath. We never got hurt, but we always knew we might. We still could not name them, though we looked them up on our computers at home, drew sketches on the screen, asked for definitions.

We decided, one day, to bring the schoolchildren. We were a long time coming to this decision: what if the children scared the animals or the animals the children? What if our place was ruined by the visit? What if someone was hurt and we were sued?

But days in the classroom, we couldn't stop seeing the animal in the children—how they ran with their arms pumping, tumbled, fell, got up again in the concrete play yard. How their bangs fell over their eyes as they leaned into their computer screens. How, when they cut themselves, the wounds turned, within hours, into something else: bark forming again, hair growing, new skin appearing like the satin skin on boiled milk, or the hard, glazed skin on ice. The children we taught were eight years old. We could hear them growing in our classrooms, their bones creaking, their blood coming to a rolling boil. We had no children of our own, and we loved these ones as if we had given birth to them. It will do them good, we told ourselves, to be outdoors.

But we did not take them lightly; we did not take the trip lightly. We knew this was the woods; these were city children. This was the tail, tail end of the twentieth century when, for most of us, the forest was a bright green foray through the plasma of a screen. The children didn't, most of them, know dirt, or lichen, or moss, or the way an animal can dart past you, sidle up to you, lick you, bite you, or gaze past you as if you're nothing.

We got chaperons, one for each child. Some of them were parents; some were friends. All were tall, with serious shoulders. We gave each child a number, each chaperon a number, etched on plastic bracelets on their wrists. Each pair also got a compass, a water bottle, a cellular telephone, extra socks. We talked to them before we left, all about the forest—where you could find it, what it looked like, how to walk in the woods without falling, what to do if you fell, if you got lost, what not to eat, what not to touch, what to touch.

The chaperons said, My god, you're experts, where did you learn?

No, we said, really, we're not. We've picked it up as we go along. We've read some books, seen some movies.

How did you find this place? ask the chaperons. They were looking at us half with suspicion, half with admiration and something close to desire.

One day, we said, walking.

Walking where?

We waved vaguely at the classroom, the window, the walled playground, the tall, lit city.

Out.

I cannot say what happened to the others during the day in the woods. For me, the day was much like any other I had spent there, except that I held an eight-year-old child tightly by the hand. I was chaperon to our most sickly child. In my backpack I had her pills and inhaler, as well as bandages for her cuts, an icepack for her bruises, lozenges for the roughness in her throat.

I held her hand; she looked. She wasn't afraid of the woods, but nor was she eager. She didn't speak to me. We didn't name the trees or talk about the weather. When an animal came up, I knew it was the same one we had met that very first day. This time, he was watchful, did not bound or leap. I kneeled, and he licked me once on my neck. Then he sniffed at the back of the girl's knees and turned and sidled away.

What was that? asked the girl, then, rubbing at the back of her knees.

I don't know, I said.

Why did he smell me? she asked.

To get to know you, maybe?

Then why did he leave?

I don't know.

He'll come back, she said.

That night we all gathered by the lake. The chaperons held the children on their shoulders, away from danger. It was a beautiful sight—so many strong shoulders, so many children, all ringing the lake like trees. We stood there for a long time. I could feel the child on my shoulders, idly playing with my hair. It was as if we had gathered by the lake to drink, but then forgotten our original purpose. We didn't talk to each other or face each other. We spread out all around the edge of the lake, like beacons. We stood.

I saw the girl running down the bank out of the corner of my eye—a tiny movement on the horizon, something I might just as well have missed. But I saw her, and turned, and knew she wasn't one of ours, since every pair of shoulders held a child. She wasn't one of ours, but she might have been, in her hot pink jacket and purple leggings, her blue sneakers, moving in a streak of color toward the lake.

Stop!

I may have yelled it, or someone else may have. I ran for her, and behind me I could feel all the other grown-ups running, our necks stretched forward, our legs pushing, stop stop, the children tumbling from our backs. But by the time I got to her, she was underwater, barely a clot of color.

I pulled her from the lake by her sodden, pink hood, placed her face-down on the bank, and opened her mouth to let the water out. We flipped her over. One person took off her shoes and rubbed her feet. Another took off her pants and spread greasy ointment on her skin. There she was, in front of us—a homo sapiens, a child, a girl, intricate and alive. There she was, breathing, the tendons in her neck rising, her belly rising, each hair on her body standing up in the wind and chill and growing dark.

Looking at her, we must have forgotten about the other children, the ones we had come with. One man took off his jacket and covered her in it. Another took an extra pair of socks from his backpack, and we pulled them up her short, brown legs like bandages. We sat her up and she looked around at us, blinking, water running out her ears and mouth.

By the time we turned around to look, something had happened. Either the lake had risen, lapping up to their feet, and then their waists and necks, or else the children—thirsty, parched with longing—had gone down to the water and entered it.

We turned and saw how they were all half-gone—how one boy's blue jacket was barely out of sight; how another child had shed her clothes on the shore, leaving her things in a muddled heap. We did not know if they were swimming (these children who had never before seen a lake) or sinking downward to the bottom. We did not know if they had gone in of their own free will or been pulled there by some reaching arm, some tide. It was dark by then; we could only see in glimpses, if at all.

I called for the sick child, my charge, but she was nowhere to be seen. We pulled out our cell phones and called into the city. Send helicopters, we said. And dogs. Send help. Some of us dove and found nothing. The water closed in front of us, a face determined to reveal nothing.

Then we sat down, for there was nothing else to do, and the girl we had pulled from the water sat with us and hummed, and we didn't know whether to be angry with her, for she had made us lose sight of the others, or grateful to her for still breathing—her coughs, sniffles and sneezes noises we knew in the night.

I wanted the animal to come and comfort me, nose his snout beneath my arm, surprising me from behind. I wanted his bristly bulk to settle in my lap; I might sleep there, my head on his back, feeling how he was me and was not me, timing my breath to his.

The helicopters got there first. It was the sort of tragedy the papers loved: *Field Trip Gone Awry; Lake Swallows Children. Reality Worse Than Virtual Reality. Stay inside*, they warned us. *Stay in.*

We lost our jobs and lost our children.

Now, sometimes, I go to the virtual woods, enter the lush greens and drunken purples of tropical rain forests, or the burning, metallic golds of a New England fall. Never are the woods the way they were that day—ordinary, off-season, slick and moldy and filled with children, hiding a creature I could not name but had grown to love. Still, I find something like pleasure in the woods on my screen, something like solace. Someone has imagined these places. Someone has been there.

For months, now, I have lived inside a grief thicker and less bearable than any place I've ever been. Still my blood flows, still my eyes blink, still my breath comes in and out. Still my tongue struggles toward something like speech in this edgy, bony, difficult, surprising world.

Susannah Breslin

Susannah Breslin grew up in Berkeley, California. She's a high school dropout who now holds an advanced degree and recently acquired a real job with stockings, skirts, and everything! She has collected her stories under the title *Pleasures of a Sandpaper Tongue.*

Apartment

He was down on the rug with the dog and he had started with the first one holding it between his fingers and then moving it around. "Boobs, boobs" he said under his breath and moved down to the next one on the dog's stomach. They were nice. His mother was in the doorway watching him and he was on the next one and it came out of his mouth again. "Boobs" saying how it felt in his hand. It was like the time he had touched the babysitter's breasts when his father had given him money to kiss her in front of the camera. Once, he had tried to put his tongue in her mouth but she had gotten really mad and told him not to do it again not EVER. Her face had been a tight ball.

Now his girlfriend was on all fours in front of him and he was fucking her. He had his hand pushing down on the small part of her back so his dick was hitting her harder and better and higher up. "Boobs" it had come out of his mouth and she was trying to turn around toward him and saying "Huh?" He thought about how he could take his dick out of her and just ram it up her ass and she wouldn't be able to do much but maybe take in a lot of breath real quick. He could tell her it was an accident. His dick had slipped. He closed his eyes and pretended he was fucking the old babysitter. He opened his eyes and the girlfriend was still there with her butt bopping forward every time he went up into her. His dick was getting limp.

He lay down on the bed and his dick got hard again so that it was up on his stomach. His girlfriend was still on her hands and knees with her butt in the air and her face on the pillow turned away from him. It looked like she was waiting for him. He got back up behind her and his dick started to get limp again. It was really

115

pissing him off. He lay down and it was hard again. He got back up really fast and tried to get in her before it had a chance to realize what he was doing. It shrank faster and when he pushed it up to her quick it crumpled back on him.

"I am going to make dinner," she said to him lying on her back. She appeared to be addressing the ceiling but she was probably telling this to him. "I could help you," he said. He was lying on his stomach, looking at the side of her face that was closest to him. He watched her heart moving her left breast up and down. She had small tits and he thought about raising his left arm up and letting his hand fall down onto her tit and seeing if he could flatten it all the way. It would make a slappy meat sound. He thought that after she left she would jack off at home. If he put his hand up and further back towards the wall and let it fall it would land on her face. That would make a harder hitting sound. Her mouth would get all mashed up against her teeth but he wouldn't be able to see that with his hand in the way.

She got up and put on a t-shirt and boxers from his drawer. She went to the refrigerator and began taking things out that he couldn't identify because they were all in bags or containers. She took something out of a bag and started messing with it. He found his underwear in the sheets at the bottom of the bed and put them on and went into the kitchen and stood next to her. The food had been taken out of the bags and she had opened the containers. She had put a big knife out onto the counter. He looked at it. He had one hand in his shorts cupping his balls with his palm.

He took his girlfriend's hand away from the food and put it on the counter and started moving the knife with the point down in between her fingers doing Mumbly Peg. The point was hitting the counter between her spread out fingers and making a banging noise. He did it faster. She leaned towards him and screamed loud in his ear high and short so he stopped and she went back to the food. He thought he saw her roll her eyes out the window to the people in the apartment on the other side of the street. They were all standing together behind the blinds lined up and looking out so you couldn't see them except for their eyes. There were two pairs of eyes up high and two down low that were the kids looking out. She picked up a cucumber and began peeling it into the sink. He left her moving stuff around in the kitchen and went into the bathroom. He pulled his dick out of his underwear and stood back against the wall to see if he could pee into the toilet from that far. It made a loud noise and splashed up on the seat some. If she had to go to the bathroom she would either sit in the wet pee if she went soon or put her butt onto the dried-up pee on the seat if she did it later. One time he had gotten up in the middle of the night at her house still drunk from the bar they had been to. He couldn't find her bathroom in the dark so he went back into the corner between the bookcase and the wall. He leaned with his head on a shelf and peed onto her rug until he couldn't go anymore. She hadn't said anything about it yet and he had done it about two months ago.

He saw that the garbage can in the bathroom was overflowing. There were towels and clothes on the floor. He took the wastebasket from the bathroom and went out the back door and down the stairs to the back alley. Dumping the trash into the big can he watched as a bunch of little white bundles fell in. There were about four carefully wrapped packages going from the basket into the bigger container. She had been having her period until a few days ago and he knew that what was in them had to do with that. He put the lid back on the can and checked to see if anyone had been watching. It was possible that the slats of the blinds across the street had been spread apart from people looking out. He wasn't sure. He thought he had seen the curtains in the lower apartment moving around but that could have been from the wind. Or maybe someone had fallen down just then and grabbed at the edges of the drapes to catch themselves but had missed and hit their head into the edge of the window on the way down to the floor. He couldn't tell.

When he got back up into the apartment the girlfriend had one pot and one pan boiling on the stove and she had finished making the salad. "I am making soup," she told him. She didn't say what was in the pan but he guessed it was meat. She put her hands palm down out over the stove as if she was keeping it down with her hands. She turned and walked back into the bathroom and closed the door behind her. The door stuck so she had to close it again and slam it hard to wedge it closed. Standing in the kitchen next to the stove he could feel the heat coming off onto his stomach. He was still in his underwear and he realized that he had gone and taken the trash out in only his shorts.

He picked the lid up off the soup and looked inside. It was thick and yellowish with pieces of vegetable in it. He leaned over to the sink from where he was standing and got the container of liquid detergent that was there. He turned it upside down over the pot and poured some of it in. There was a white spot that was the detergent in the middle of the soup so he used a spoon to stir it in. The color of the soup was now a lighter yellow. He put the lid back on and sat down at the table until the girlfriend came out and put the salad and a hamburger on the plate in front of him. She set a bowl of soup next to the big plate with the vegetable and meat but the girlfriend did not give herself any soup. He began eating the salad and hamburger and spoons of the soup in turns one after the other. The soup tasted a little soapy so he held the other food in his mouth and ate it all together with his nose plugged and then it tasted better.

When they had eaten everything she said, "I think I better go." "I think you'd better go," he told her. She had put all her clothes on and was ready to leave so he walked with her to the door. He opened it for her and she kissed him goodbye on the mouth. He could see that the eye of the man in the apartment across the hall was pressed up against the glass of his peephole. The eye was wide open and bulging out the hole so it made a bump on the door. When the girlfriend walked out the door he closed it on her so that she was caught between the door and the frame around it. Her arm below the elbow was sticking out into the apartment so the door did not entirely shut. Her fingers were moving around and he could now see her in the hall through his own peephole and she was undoing her pants with her other hand. He saw she was going to masturbate in the hall if she wasn't able to get home soon. Her one hand went into her pants while the other one opened and closed trying to get out from in the door.

If the dog had been there he could yell for it to sic and it would jump up and hang by its teeth from her arm. He leaned towards her hand where it was feeling up and down the side of the door for the doorknob. He bit the forearm near the wrist and the hand turned around towards him and tried to grab at his face but it couldn't maneuver much between the door and the wall. What was he going to do? It kept looking for ways to get out and he could hear the eye of the man across the hall breathing deep and hard. He knew the big knife was in the kitchen and he suddenly tried to run for it and get back in time before the hand knew he was gone. He ran through the apartment and made a small u-turn in the kitchen to pick up the knife without even stopping. He ran faster in his underwear it seemed. But back at the door the hand was gone and had even closed the door shut carefully and quietly behind it. At the window over the sink he could see her walking away and he threw the knife out the window at her. It fell down into the bushes underneath him.

Sandy Huss

Sandy Huss teaches fiction writing at the University of Alabama
at Tuscaloosa. Her first book, *Labor for Love: Stories,* was published by the University of Missouri Press in 1992. The piece in
this volume is an excerpt from *Scrapbook,* a novel in progress;
other excepts have appeared in the anthology *Lesbian Erotics,*
edited by Karla Jay; and in *two girls review.*

@work.edu

have a job -- and it might be their last one. It's their decision, in theory, whether or not to wade ever again into an applicant pool. Troubled waters, those: the swimming's hardly synchronized, no buddy system's in effect, and the life guards' eyes have long since sealed themselves tightly against the glare coming off the whitesoastobetakenseriouslynographicgestureseitheri'mserioushererepleasejustgivemeabreakandTAKEME resumes. ✄ were buoyed the last time they took a dip in this soup, kept afloat by an identity: they look a certain way,

It's up to you to be creative and experiment, and as always, avoid accidents by passing scissors by the handle

sound a certain way, have official documents certifying their right to claim a supposedly certain something. Like the raft of inoculations a lucky infant gets in order to increase its chances on the planet, this earmark cut ✄ into the loop and kept them viable. Since they need a job, they're grateful that this profile has its hip demographic coordinates, happy to carry its card. The down side is that it's as likely to do you in as to immunize you. Like lots of identities. Maybe all of them. ✄ have a long history with this role, and a big hunk of that relationship is martial:

shuss

Editors: *12 Ounce Prophet*, Vol.1, #2

G

R A

P P L

I N G I R

O N S S H O U

L D N E V E R B E

P L A C E D W H E R E

T H E Y A R E E X P O S E

D T O P U B L I C V I E W

f i -
nally, it's
not a shoe that
really fits. Not that
they've known many shoes
to fit, even the ones that more
or less do. If you've got the
cash, it's great to have several pair so that you can switch
them out when they start to
hobble you. ✂ could even
sympathize with somebody
who thought they needed two
separate pair of green suede
jobs with black plastic zippers:
the differences might be
subtle, but last they heard,
subtlety still had its partisans.
The truth is, ✂ go barefoot as
much as possible. Still, if they
have to be a white female
wearing corrective lenses in
order to drive a car, a white
female wearing corrective
lenses they'll be. It might not
have been an identity that
eventually got them hired, but
without it they wouldn't have
been: they'll sport its brand in-
definitely. As long as they
work here -- and did they men-
tion they could work here

The American National Red Cross:
Life Saving and Water Safety, 1968

for-
ever? --
they will be
hated for it (loved!),
dismissed because of it (rewarded!), handicapped by it
(enabled!). It might not have
been this stamp that secured
their job for life and changed
the name of their rank -- but it
could be construed that way.
This makes ✂ feel like a
fraud, but not because they're
worried about stacking up:
merit's always shod in its
moment's fashion. As jobs go,
✂ might have done far worse.
Have -- in their past. Here, at
least, the hours are somewhat
flexible, there's no heavy lifting, and the benefits package
almost makes up for the lousy
pay. Which is nonetheless
better than most people can
expect. But a certain kind of
excitement's in short supply:
there's no call for adrenaline.
Unless, of course, you don't
like what ✂ stand for. In that
case you're always on alert to
discover what they and their
cohort must be plotting.

They
must
have an
identity: they
feel something
trying to kill
them: they're
a Target,
therefore
they Are. The
postures
they've
assumed over
time have
hung around
in the same
bars, eaten
out of the
same box of
Cheerios, run
in the same
10K's: wher-
ever one of
them is,
another lurks,
or is bound to
show up soon
-- they're

accumu-
lating mass
and predict-
ability. It
feels like life
in a MASH unit,
a big red
crosshair
blazoned on
one of the
tents: some
war or another
has produced
them as
casualties and
is out to finish
them off. They
resuscitated a
body once.
When it came
to, it bit them.
Hard.

fox&geese

On a certain TV drama, the workers run pell mell, pushing patients on gurneys, spewing data and diagnoses, wielding syringes and plastic tubing -- sometimes leaping aboard the moving cart and straddling a body -- their anatomical and technological muscle all aflex. ✕ (who aren't scheming anything but how soon they can take a trip to Florida where there's a lottery) have been heard to say that their own job's a lark in comparison. The only time they've ever seen anyone around here break a legitimate sweat, their colleagues were in route to Marta's funeral. Marta's hire was colored in a way ✕ can relate to: her identity affirmed their institution's commitment to Diversity. And the word was that she'd taken her own life on account of the disdainful and derogatory and denigrating way she'd been treated by her rank superiors. With whom, it is to be supposed, she at some time in her life identified. It's funny how certain two-way streets can, whenever school's in session, become strictly unidirectional. Two people are running to the ritual, galloping down the stairs. They're late getting out of a meeting: meetings have so much power that sometimes not even the powerful can stop them. The running woman is ✕'s boss, boss of their whole division. The running man works for her too, even though he outranks her: don't let that Senior Professor badge on his sleeve confuse you the way it sometimes confuses him. The boss's trench coat billows like an academic gown and the Senior Professor's jacket vents are flapping -- each has their watch arm up as a warning to the stairwell's other occupants: out of the way! out of the way! we're your emissaries to a terrible ceremony! Except that one of them isn't ✕'s representative at all. One of them will never say a word to ✕ about Marta's burial.

afog,eden,sex

124

They first read The Great Woolfy for Madonna's class
when they were in college. They love
how VW reels it out, and even
how she reels it in --
all the while claiming
you shouldn't
ought to.

IN THOSE DAYS -- THE LAST OF QUEEN VICTORIA -- EVERY HOUSE HAD ITS ANGEL. AND WHEN I CAME TO WRITE I ENCOUNTERED HER WITH THE VERY FIRST WORDS. THE SHADOW OF HER WINGS FELL ON MY PAGE; I HEARD THE RUSTLING OF HER SKIRTS IN THE ROOM. DIRECTLY, THAT IS TO SAY, I TOOK MY PEN IN HAND TO REVIEW THAT NOVEL BY A FAMOUS MAN, SHE SLIPPED BE-HIND ME AND WHISPERED: "MY DEAR, YOU ARE A YOUNG WOMAN. YOU ARE WRITING ABOUT A BOOK THAT HAS BEEN WRITTEN BY A MAN. BE SYMPATHETIC; BE TENDER; FLATTER; DECEIVE; USE ALL THE ARTS AND WILES OF OUR SEX. NEVER LET ANYBODY GUESS THAT YOU HAVE A MIND OF YOUR OWN. ABOVE ALL, BE PURE." AND SHE MADE AS IF TO GUIDE MY PEN. I NOW RECORD THE ONE ACT FOR WHICH I TAKE SOME CREDIT TO MYSELF, THOUGH THE CREDIT RIGHTLY BELONGS TO SOME EXCELLENT ANCESTORS OF MINE WHO LEFT ME A CERTAIN SUM OF MONEY -- SHALL WE SAY FIVE HUNDRED POUNDS A YEAR? -- SO THAT IT WAS NOT NECESSARY FOR ME TO DEPEND SOLELY ON CHARM FOR MY LIVING. I TURNED UPON HER AND CAUGHT HER BY THE THROAT. I DID MY BEST TO KILL HER. MY EXCUSE, IF I WERE TO BE HAD UP IN A COURT OF LAW, WOULD BE THAT I ACTED IN SELF-DEFENCE. HAD I NOT KILLED HER SHE WOULD HAVE KILLED ME. SHE WOULD HAVE PLUCKED THE HEART OUT OF MY WRITING. FOR, AS I FOUND, DIRECTLY I PUT PEN TO PA-PER, YOU CANNOT REVIEW EVEN A NOVEL WITHOUT HAVING A MIND OF YOUR OWN, WITHOUT EXPRESSING WHAT YOU THINK TO BE THE TRUTH ABOUT HUMAN RELATIONS, MORALITY, SEX. AND ALL THESE QUESTIONS, ACCORDING TO THE ANGEL IN THE HOUSE, CANNOT BE DEALT WITH FREELY AND OPENLY BY WOMEN; THEY MUST CHARM, THEY MUST CONCILIATE, THEY MUST -- TO PUT IT BLUNTLY -- TELL LIES IF THEY ARE TO SUCCEED. THUS, WHENEVER I FELT THE SHADOW OF HER WING OR THE RADIANCE OF HER HALO UPON MY PAGE, I TOOK UP THE INKPOT AND FLUNG IT AT HER. SHE DIED HARD. HER FICTITIOUS NA-TURE WAS OF GREAT ASSISTANCE TO HER. IT IS FAR HARDER TO KILL A PHANTOM THAN A REALITY.

Virginia Woolf: "Professions for Women"

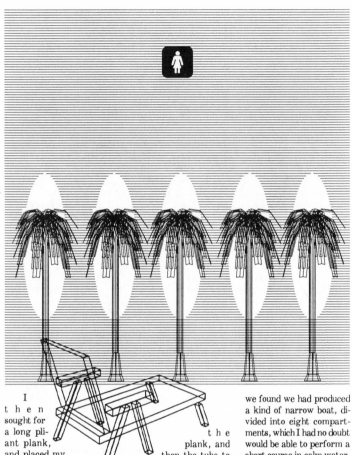

I then sought for a long pliant plank, and placed my eight tubs upon it, leaving a piece at each end reaching beyond the tubs, which, bent upward, would present an outline like the keel of a vessel; we next nailed all the tubs to the plank, and then the tubs to each other, as they stood, side by side, to make them the firmer, and afterwards two other planks, of the same length as the first, on each side of the tubs. When all this was finished, we found we had produced a kind of narrow boat, divided into eight compartments, which I had no doubt would be able to perform a short course in calm water.

But now we discovered that the machine we had contrived was so heavy, that, with the strength of all united, we were not able to move it an inch from its place.

David Wyss: *The Swiss Family Robinson*
As retold by Mabel Dodge Holmes, Ph.D., Teacher of English,
William Penn High School, Philadelphia, c. 1929

You could say that the funeral is turning into a sideshow: ✂ want to claim it as the main event. Suspect their motives for this emphasis, if you like: it's true that they have the occasional ulterior fantasy. They dream of getting out of this racket, of producing their own show on TV, an hour-long drama for which Marta's given them a great idea. The Survivors,

> Marta was alone in the world: she left it a house. A five room house with a Christmas tree in every room. Five rooms, five trees, five angels hovering. Garlands, lights, tinsel -- the works. Ornaments that had lasted. Ornaments that were new. Catalogue expensive. Drugstore cheap. The tasteless and what passes for the tasteful too. Marta's arms raised. Marta crouching, Marta standing back to judge the effect. Marta squinting, moving this Guatemalan pony next to this Indian bell next to this Mexican cow next to this icicle from Finland. Marta flicking her fingers against the bubble lights to set them in motion. Marta carrying water, arranging the trees' skirts.

shoes are perched on a podium. Just as they are here, at Marta's funeral. The guy doing her eulogy, one of her mentors -- from a different (in name at least) institution -- brought Marta's shoes with h i m , s p e a k s o v e r them, as if they were her very body. This guy isn't wearing heels, that's for sure -- he's not s a y i n g anything mincing. Not allow-

they'd call it, and it would open each week with a computer-synthesized murmuring behind the credits: tossmethatbonei'llearnyourrespect-GETALIFEwhydon'tyou? A nice tight shot on a pair of size 9 heels. Then the camera backs up, and you see that the

ing for trouble in Marta's past, not spinning any mumbo jumbo about glitches in chemical circuitry. He's out and out accusing Marta's colleagues of murder. He taught her well, see, taught her everything he knew. He thinks she's been treated unfairly.

127

✂ know that he's one of the good guys, just like that well-meaning Senior Professor -- who's sitting scandalized (titillated!), solemn (licentious!), and erect (you bet!) down front there in his serious Sunday suit. The trouble with all the good guys is that they hold onto the Guy part and leave ✂ no choice but to be a Gal and strap on their spikes. The world is more than half full of Martas after all, and somebody oughta learn them how to bait a hook. If ✂ mistake anybody for a worm and impale them in the process, it's just an accident, nothing personal: ✂'s fishing license is (alas and alack!) silent on the subject of their vision. Not, mind you, that they find the Good part any easier to swallow: a Guy's never more abrasive than when he's rehearsing what he's gained through laborious and brow-beaten study. That just makes ✂ snippy, makes them hanker for the way a bad guy takes his cue and snarls. Or better yet, for something The Bomb once did, on a day when ✂ wore their cowboy boots with steel toe-tips to a meeting. (Some terrain is as treacherous as a sidewalk grate, and ✂ are, occasionally, prudent.) The Bomb went down on his hands and knees and put his puckered lips to the polished metal: objective correlative! symbol! emotion recollected in tranquillity! ✂ have never seen such a poetic expression. Their only bitch is that The Bomb waited until the meeting was over. But ✂ aren't here to bitch. That's not at all what they're doing. If anything, they're playing a lyre: they like the way it sounds, the lyre. They hope somebody plays one at their funeral.

apparently it isn't easy to like a person who isn't humbled by second place

Alice Walker, in her dedication to *I Love Myself When I Am Laughing And Then Again When I Am Looking Mean and Impressive: A Zora Neale Hurston Reader*

BOOTJACK

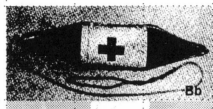

Bb

BUOYS
(A. lighted whistle; B,
lighted; C, whistling; D,
bell; E. nun; F. spar; G, can)

*They're not Type A; that's for sure, but
does that make them Type B -- stolid,
unflappable, steady in an emergency?
They might have said sure, it's obvious
-- until recently -- when they started
dreaming of going postal, started
plotting their weapon, their footwear,
their itinerary.*

S.W.A.K.

) afloat; usually with a
o lift up or keep up i
ts; encourage; usual

The World Publishing Company:
Webster's New World Dictionary
The American National Red Cross:
Life Saving & Water Safety, 1968

Rikki Ducornet

Rikki Ducornet's fifth novel, *Philosopher in Dreamland*, was named a Best Book of the Year by *Publisher's Weekly* and received the Critic's Circle Award for 1995. She is published by Dalkey Archive Press and lives in Denver.

The Many Tenses of Wanting

I have come to you with the expectation that together we will sever the knot of my perplexed (my perpetual!) infancy.

Weighted down by virtual baggage, I am not—as you noted instantly—an autonomous being and autonomy is precisely what I am wanting. However, I have what you call a sexual soul, or rather, the capacity to evolve into a sexual being, to reveal an authentic blue streak, the capacity not only to inspire but to withstand heat, to weather my stripes and to shed my old skin. I intend to astonish us both.

You asked me any number of things; you startled me. Almost at once my heart quickened with something like hope: Is he really after the truth? Is he able to look into the darkest corners of the heart without flinching? The man is no prude, I thought, and furthermore he is smart. And good-looking. Sumerian! A Semitic face, the beard threaded with silver, nose prominent, eyes deepest black. Not that I—supine on the little couch and staring at the ceiling in the classic pose—got to see much of your face!

Again: You asked me any number of things—all interesting and necessary, and this *despite the risks* you described, or, as you so engagingly revealed to me—*because of the risks implied*. Obviously, as you pointed out, there is always danger when the engagement is acute. As in passionate loving. *We are talking about real life here*, you said; *that is the intention of the work we have undertaken together*.

A thrilling phrase! I think of Houdini unpuzzling his chains and rising to the surface of his man-size aquarium. *Undertaken together!* I shall help you rob my own grave so that I may steal away with my own intrinsic capacity *to be someone*. It occurs to me that to engage in the world of the living one *must be prompt*. If only because there is so little time. (And yet there you sit, Doctor, greying at the temples. Don't you hear the winds of time raging about your little office in the sky?)

I have always been sluggish. Although my infancy was punctuated by my mother's rallying cry: *step on it*! I misunderstood. I thought that time was to be killed, crushed beneath the foot like a centipede else it leap to my leg and inflict a mortal sting. I imagined wasting away. You evoked Plotinus and Jung simultaneously when you added: *each memory, dream, and reflection must inform the immediate present. We are,* you said also, *about to confront the chaos of cryptic language. But rest assured: the characters, runes, wedges, hieroglyphs, whatever—all mean something.* And so: the vortex I carry within me, just as chaos itself, is simply an undeciphered, an uncharted system.

* * *

My first memories are of such uncharted and undeciphered spaces, of a white light which was the sky over Iran, a brilliant light illuminating particles of dust. I was, perhaps, three or four and had no notion of numbers but surely a sense of the infinite because I recall that sky and those reeling particles with an extreme fear as though I could be swallowed up in such a swarming. The world revealed itself to me at that moment and for the first time. My senses were accosted on all sides at once and so great was that swarming in my mind that to this day I believe I saw a man with the head of a camel and a donkey with a man's body and as alive as you and I.

My father was president of both the American Bible Society and a soft drink company; he hoped to convince his Iranian hosts of the inevitability of Christ and carbonated coffee. He failed, but even now the short years we spent in Iran animate my dreams. For example, I have a recurrent dream of a bazaar in which upon the unpaved dirt all things of significance are laid out—not only dates and sugarcane but ideas: the idea of color and the idea of music;

flavors, also, the gummy eyes of children going blind, luxurious grief and violent anger, passionate love and wickedness, fragments of poetry, the Supreme Deity (and he is a cherub with the body of a bull and the head of a man), the Fall of Man, the cattle of the field, the pine tree of Eridu, the severed head of our servant—his name was Hadji—Hadji's head displayed like a geographer's plaster model, his ruined eye a volcano, the scar (from temple to chin) a river of fire. Although it was not Hadji's head that was cut off but his hand—for he had stolen a box of Bisquick from my mother's kitchen. My father attempted to beg for leniency, but by preparing American pancakes for his family in his hovel, Hadji had dishonored his country. So that the final months in Iran were marked by shame and horror and all the ensuing hocus-pocus; my parents, motivated by dread, argued the Bible's most cryptic passages and then Mother fled the ancient world for the new in a fit of loathing (and she took me with her).

Another early memory (and this before I was to learn of Hadji's downfall) is of a visit to the vanished Tower of Babel in a heat so intense I was stricken with fever and nearly died; the little cotton kerchief my mother had tied about my head doing nothing to protect me from the furious eye of the sun. And—is it surprising—for days I spoke in a confusion of tongues. I sounded like a Finn speaking about Babylonian legal codes in Turkish was my mother's joke. My mother was a wit—far too smart for father whose mind plodded at best. But even though we left Iran when I was not yet nine, I still believe, deep in my soul, that the stars, the moon, and sun rule over our days and nights. I mean I cannot look at them without shuddering as though they were so many feral creatures threatening to sever my limbs with one bite should I fail to pay attention, fail to be on time. I'm always in a panic I'll miss something essential. For example, I noticed your habit of caressing your lower lip with the knuckle of your left index finger—a charming gesture, seductive, actually (and this is why I recall the things you said so clearly). And I think there may be a key here—some sort of explanation as to why I am so *consummately*

Babylonian in my neurotic comportment—I am making reference here to my habits—*obsessions* if you will: there are days when I dare not remove my clothes, or wear white, or speak in public, or take medicine, or utter a curse. This is why I have come to you. It has become increasingly difficult for me to function in the world. Last week I was unable to utter a word; I was afraid of being sexually penetrated by moonlight, by the volatile essences of plants and the vapor of the bath.

* * *

I was told that you are "a man of spirit" and I have not been disappointed. Our first meeting was, to my mind, exceptional. Until now my therapists have all been hand-holders, potential thugs or mystics. You will not attempt to bludgeon me with terminology, demand that I worship in the Holy Temple of Freud, look for the goddess within, mother me, seduce me—*or allow me to seduce you*—for, as you noted, I am a pretty woman, youthful for my age and due to my diminutive size and Oriental features (my mother was Japanese) doll-like, even—a thing that endears me to older men.

And because I am somehow *intact* (and now we come to the heart of the matter), having—in the sexual act—always managed *to be elsewhere*, I fascinate many men (and women too); they pride themselves in this way: they think they will be the one to awaken me. But no one has. I may spend hours altogether gazing at images of lust, for example the Babylonian figures of Enkidu and the whore copulating shamelessly, limbs spread, tense, contorted, in collision like forces of nature.... Or I read the little sonnets of the Renaissance: *Open your thighs so I can look straight at your beautiful* culo *and* potta *before my face* and so on—without being aroused. In fact, it is a game I play with myself, to look upon these things with disinterest, coolly, as one might examine the sexual encounters of fish. And yet I am certain that it could be otherwise and wish it were so, for my loneliness is intolerable and I fear I shall become a hag of ice—if I am not that already.

To continue: I am assured having met with you once that between the two of us—despite a powerful attraction on my part—because yes, I am capable of feeling attraction and relish the chase (an attraction that has more to do with affinities than transference—it is far too soon to speak of transference!)—there will be no foolishness! You will not step across the Ispahan that separates us like a sea to embrace me. I will not hear you whisper: *Open your thighs so I can look straight at your beautiful* culo *and* potta *before my face.* I will not see ardor in your eyes, nor will you in mine. More's the pity. We will engage in matters of the spirit, only. Despite the affinities that clearly exist (after an hour, only! An hour!) between our bodies and our souls. (For it is possible and the irony here is unbearable—that you—in other circumstances—could be the one to awaken me. How sweet it would be to long for you!) But there will be no love-making. Your rigor in such matters is exemplary. Your high social character. Your sound judgment and moral worth. Your marriage, the children of college age—I have done my own investigating—all this has decided me to come to you. After so many failures. Yes. You will give me a *sexual soul*— as you put it—but not by fucking me. Although, as I have said, so many find me irresistible. And this because I am the bright mirror of desire; I am like a clay that is never touched by fire and so may be modeled again and again. (This said, I bruise easily. A lover once left parallel thumbprints on the inside of both my knees and beneath each buttock. My skin so white the marks blue—a strange tattoo. How beautiful I looked after! How mysterious! I crawled up on the bathroom sink, my buttocks to the glass, and gazed at those two marks, at my ass, my cunt beneath, imagining that I was my own lover. *Open your thighs so I* . . . Any other woman would have been dizzied by the sight!)

* * *

Even in my infancy I was beautiful. In Babylon, Hadji

135

proposed daily that I should be rolled in powdered sugar and eaten with a spoon. Once when we traveled *en famille* in a *kooffah*—so like a wooden bowl floating in the water—his conceit seemed so apt it terrified me. I was in the bowl—where was Hadji's spoon?

Hadji told great stories. My favorite was about the caliph al-Mamoon who showered his bride with pearls. Living in a household rigorous in the denial of luxury and pleasure, how could the story not impress me? Ever since Hadji and my time in Babylon, sugar is not sweet enough, nor red red enough. No man will spill pearls on *my* head! Although I expect your words, Doctor, will be that precious, that illuminating. You see—I expect wonders of another sort from you, from us; yes: our minds will catch fire. My eternal winter will quicken into spring and I shall know summer and I shall know what it is to live in the world, to live in a body.

After Hadji lost his hand and we prepared to depart from Iran, father projected a voyage to distant lands even beyond Ethiopia. He explained that the people living there were without lineage and had no knowledge of the Flood. A people without knowledge of the Flood! A people like a clean, soft clay upon whom he could impress his idea of the divine. He would tame them with the fear of Jehovah and civilize them with coffee cola. He would set a holy fire beneath their seats and precipitate them into industrious bees in a hive of his own making.

Imagine! Heathens dressed in overalls reciting the Lord's Prayer while drinking soda pop—while *producing* soda pop! He would be the Henry Ford of Nubia! He would precipitate an entire race into history. He would introduce them to the Flood: the ebb and tide of capital! Already imagining his advertising campaign—*The only cola made with God's own rain!*—he imagined cisterns, fields of cane sugar and hillsides green with Ethiopian coffee. Mother was silent. She knew Nubia was as arid as her own life.

You can tell that Father was not much of a reader—apart from the Bible, his accounting books, his well-thumbed copy of Burkitt's *Climate, Costs, and Coffee*. What he knew about the world he had learned in Sunday school. Often he was irked by what he called Mother's *Japanese queerness.* (You are wondering how they met: at a church supper in Flushing, New York.) Mother now said: *Cola has failed in Mesopotamia. Why should it flourish in Nubia?* Father replied: *A question of faith.* He had figured it all out, you see: God had purposely made the business fail, had even tempted Hadji's greed *so that we should move on*—a remark that put my mother irremediably out of patience. She said: *I don't think God gives a fig for soda pop, or a fig for Nubians either, for that matter.* And she had refused to follow him. The last we heard he had entered a bugless land of blasted rock that stretched towards infinity beneath a sapphire-blue sky. Like a man from an earlier age, Father had set off with a case of Bibles. At some point he bought a rug and managed to post it. I still have it—a rug woven by the people for whom it is heresy to portray anything recognizable. Yet in those strenuous geometries I can see figures hiding and it seems to me that they are sexual, that the rug is a species of star chart of erotic associations. I am certain that had Father *looked* at the rug he would not have bought it. After that we never heard from him again.

We were living in Manhattan. Mother had two ribs removed and became an exotic dancer with a very small waist. Once she awakened wildly laughing, having dreamed Father was a centipede beetling his way across an infinity of rubble bringing Bibles to people who worshiped anthills. Before she died—having made a name for herself in that curious milieu she had chosen (there's a portrait of her by Pinsky in the Hines)—she told me: *Your father was the biggest bore and the greatest fool I ever knew.*

And she dreamed of Hadji—a nightmare I share (and I don't know who dreamed it first)—of Hadji's hand rigid in the sky—horizontal—rather like an oddly shaped dirigible—pointing toward a black cloud (Father's black Africa) and Father's certain death. *A man who dreamed of soda pop,* Mother said, *and who probably died of thirst.* Poor Father. A zealot and a hayseed with imperialist dreams. *He was like coffee cola,* Mother said; *an undrinkable mixture.*

* * *

I believe it is so that one's sexuality is fixed at an early age. One is impressionable and a visual experience has the impress of a firebrand. I mean one can see something so puissant it sets the mind on fire, an inextinguishable fire that—if it cools to embers with the passage of hours and days—can be rekindled by a random word.

One day in Babylon, Hadji proposed a tour of the restricted quarters of the city. Mother took to the idea and suggested we disguise ourselves She was a creature who loved a good joke and good time—as life without Father would reveal—and she sent Hadji to fetch some clothes for the two of us. I wore one of Hadji's shirts—it fell to my ankles (for Hadji was a broad, a robust man)—and put my beach sandals on; to assure the effect, Mother cut my hair. A tomboy, I was delighted to see all my curls gathering in a heap on the floor, although Hadji, distressed by the amplitude of my mother's enthusiasm, mournfully cried: *Pity! Pity!* with each snip of scissors. Seeing that he looked at the hair with longing as well as regret, Mother bent down and retrieved one curl. I laughed when he put it to his lips and kissed it, laughed to feel my naked neck in the morning breeze, to see myself transformed into an Arab boy. In Hadji's long coat, turban, and scarves, Mother looked positively *calif.*

Doctor. Not a night passes without my dreaming of that morning. I dream of fractured cobbled paths, of palaces leaning over the street, and sudden courtyards. Free of Father for the day and feeling festive, we tasted everything: cakes as yellow as pollen, preserved apricots, buffalo cream thick and sweetened with Syrian honey.

Now you are truly seeing my country, Hadji exclaimed, and Mother said (and I had never seen her so happy) *I* love *your country!* She bit into an apricot and honey spilled down her chin. And I, intoxicated by her buoyancy, by the mysteries offered everywhere I looked, ran off into an *impasse* hung with wet silk; I ran until I came to an elaborately carved gate. I recognized honeysuckle vines and fruits—the "sacred tree" of the Assyrians. Through the intercesses of the vines I could discern a courtyard of blue and turquoise tiles shining from a recent washing. Beyond the courtyard was an open door and on the lintel stood a beautiful woman, her robe open to reveal the deep cleft of her breasts, her nipples stained red, the black moss of her pubic hair. Her eyes were so black they seemed to shadow her face. She was smoking and daydreaming and did not see me. As she lifted the cigarette to her lips I saw that her hands, too, were stained red. But then Hadji was beside me, pulling me away from the gate, then lifting me into his arms as he whispered: *Forbidden! Forbidden!* Just as he turned with me to flee from that marvelous place, I saw a painting on the wall beside the gate of an erect phallus animated by wings, a rooster-phallus ejaculating sperm in the shape of leaves and flowers.

Although I was only a slip of a girl at the time—little more than seven—I grasped what I had seen and was astonished by it. I had seen Bathsheba, I knew; I had seen through the gate of Sodom; I had seen the phallus Father had tried so hard to deny. It was the phallus a schoolmate had once drawn on the blackboard with chalk, the phallus of the winged gods of Mesopotamia.

As we burst from the alley and returned to the street where Mother was waiting gorging on fruit, I felt something thrash wildly against my ribs. It was Hadji's cock, and it startled us both. At once he set me down on my feet as I looked to his body and the place where I knew I must see something of the powerful form I had felt leaping against me. Hadji pulled his robes about him and, pretending that nothing out of the ordinary had happened, proposed lunch. He took us to a diminutive restaurant painted with birds and lions; an antique room—the paintings were faded and pocked, and this made them all the more wonderful. I felt that we had somehow entered into the sacred precincts beyond the gate, as though the forbidden space could not be circumvented because it exerted an influence upon the entire city: it was the place of the world's heartbeat and all paths led there.

Hadji ordered the best and insisted that we were his guests—although the meal must have cost him a full week's salary. Barley loaves and roasted chickens stuffed with almonds and grilled seeds, the cow's first milk after the calf is born, slices of hard, white honey. But rather than dispel the vision and the touch of Eros on fire, the feast heightened my impressions so that the forbidden moments continued to burn in my mind. The near-naked body of the mysterious whore and the body of the man Hadji took on the savors and fragrances of fruit and milk and honey. The Whore in the Courtyard, the Whore of the Full Breasts and Black Triangle—she became the image of the woman I would become, aflame in the bright light of late morning.

Doctor—can you see how that morning the incombustible palace of sex had been revealed too me in all its sumptuous mystery? Is it a wonder, Beloved Friend, that red is no longer red enough? That sugar is not sweet enough? My laughter only a seeming? How could any encounter re-create the splendor of that morning, the astonishment, the heat, the fresh knowledge of those instants?

I have taken the thrashing phallus into my mouth and tasted it blossoming there. I have taken the winged phallus into my entrails where it has reared its head and probed for my heart. Yet I remain to be awakened, for nothing has yet given back the promise of that fated morning, that terrible morning when as we left the painted room Hadji was seized, and shouting taken from us. Because a jealous neighbor had seen the strange cakes on the plate—made just as Mother had shown Hadji how to make them.

Father had been questioned in his office—had the flour, the can of Danish butter, the maple syrup been gifts? Father was shocked. Hadji had stolen—that much was clear. The devil had tempted his hand. A week passed. Mother insisted that Father intervene; Hadji's wife had come to our door, weeping. That night Father described the bandaged stump that Hadji, alone in his little cell, grieved over, holding it delicately with his left hand.

I told him to trust in God, Father said. *And he looked at me strangely. I think he is angry with me although what happened is clearly not my fault. After all, I told them to be compassionate.* Hadji, Father decided, was unlucky, but he was a thief and to have lied to the authorities to save him was unthinkable. *One does not sin for a sinner. They're all thieves,* Father decided. And he began to dream of an untouched people of clay.

I, too, dreamed of clay. As Mother and I sailed to New York City I dreamed of a clay body: malleable and insensible. Sailing a sea of lead beneath a leaden sky I thought: the one safe place is the space of an instant, an instant seized forever in a tableau of fire and ice: a fixed picture of a woman ungraspable, perceived as she dreams. And her dreams take her far, far away from the world, its terrors and losses.

* * *

Doctor, now you have it all: the enchanted island lost to sight, the voyage ever after ghostly and stark. You will say that my "all" is only the point of departure, that the voyage we have undertaken has only just begun. To tell the truth I am wild with expectation. Will you, I wonder, as tall, as broad as Hadji and despite the dangers, have the courage to give me back the fullness of that primal vision?

By the time you get this letter I will be making my way to your little anteroom where I will sit killing time with a magazine. I wonder: will you have the courage to look me in the eyes? Will you find the words? Will words be necessary?

Think of it: I am virtually that perfect creature of an Arabian night's dream. Once you have opened the gate will you be able to resist me? Would that be wise? For—and of this I am certain—together we will transcend the entire process of recovery. By the time it is over and we have given Hadji back his hand and me my heart, we will be like the first man and the first woman lying naked together; you will lean into me the way the storm leans into the trees.

Ursule Molinaro

Ursule Molinaro is the author of 11 novels (most recently *Power Dreamers*, McPherson,1994), 3 books of non-fiction (most recently *A Full Moon of Women*, Dutton 1990 & McPherson 1994), 4 collections of short stories, over 100 short stories in magazines & anthologies, and 10 one-act plays. She has published translations of novels & plays from French, German, Italian & Spanish, and has translated film subtitles from & into French and English, and from Italian. She lives in New York City.

Rat Mother

Twice a year, at the time of the equinox, in March & in September, raw eggs can stand by themselves. You place the egg, plumper side down, on a level surface   like a dining room table or a dormitory dresser   hold it gingerly between your hands until you feel the yolk settle, you withdraw your hands, & the egg stands. You feel a strange primal thrill, like seeing a bird put its head under a wing during a solar eclipse. The egg stands by itself for the duration of the equinox, unless a truck rattles past, or someone deliberately upsets the level surface.

Ramona Bear & I used to perform elaborate egg-standing rituals twice a year, during the 4 years we were college roommates. The believers would tiptoe in, & crane their necks from the door, awed by the miracle of a balanced universe in miniature, in the basic pre-commitment shape that had most likely preceded the hen. The heretics would make a rowdy entry, hoping to upset the righteous equilibrium & keep the highpriestess from repeating the feat.

They all came to the standing of the eggs, because Ramona Bear was the most beautiful woman they'd seen off screen or off stage or outside glossy fashion magazines, & they came to prove their equality, if not their superiority, to the flawless face & flawless figure they couldn't dismiss as a hollow surface. The arrogance of a beautiful woman, proclaiming that she was in love with surfaces. With proportion. Which was why she was studying to be an architect.

It thrilled her to feel an egg get ready to stand while the sun crossed the equator: she'd say to us while she performed the ritual: The ubiquitous oval of the egg, which had inspired the Arabs to invent zero. The pre-choice position between positive & negative, in which the light enfolds the dark, & no judgment is passed on either.

After college we both returned to New York City. The aspiring architect became the fashion model her fellow students always thought she ought to be. & my studies of languages, with an emphasis on etymology, qualified me for translating technical manuals.

Ramona Bear lived in stony respectability on the Upper West Side. I found a former butcher store in Greenwich Village, which a painter had converted into a studio. He had covered the walls of the toilet in black lamb fur, & gold-leafed the lion-footed bathtub in the kitchen, but had left a little yard in the back littered with rusting skeletons of bicycles, tricycles, & inner springs. Eventually, my son made it into a rock garden with small lakes full of waterlilies & salamanders.

Once a month Ramona Bear & I met halfway for lunch in a mid-town restaurant, & compared lives. Which began to show similarities we thought were beyond the promptings of biology: We married within a month of each other, produced one child the following summer—her daughter was born on July 31, my son on August 4—& divorced 11 years later, both in November.

We were friends, but not close friends. Our lunches were a non-committal constant from which we returned with regained perspective, & cheerful. She always said I made her laugh. & I enjoyed looking at her. Aging became her. At 40 she was modeling expensive coats & suits for the executive woman. A few times she sold me a piece she'd worn during a show, at a price I could afford. Beautiful clothes which I'd model for my son when I got home. My son had shown interest in what people wore since babyhood. He drew well, & at 13 he wanted to be a fashion designer. He asked me to ask Ramona Bear if she'd smuggle him into a show sometime.

I didn't want to ask her. We'd never intruded our lives on our luncheons, except as subjects of comparison & subsequent amusement. But my son insisted, & so his mother gave in. Ramona Bear thought that might be arranged. No problem. & added: That I was lucky to have a son. A daughter was her mother's nemesis. At least her daughter was.

& then she broke the tacit luncheon rule, & told me that: Since the divorce her daughter rarely spoke to her. When she did, it was with sarcastic disdain. Her daughter was deliberately destroying her body, as a judgment on her mother's superficiality.

I asked: If her daughter was on drugs.

In a way. Except that her daughter's drugs were legal. Her daughter was eating herself to death. The father was bribing the girl's affection with lavish gifts of money; as was the paternal grandmother. Her daughter was buying food with the money. Food of the most fattening kind: candy pastries cakes pizzas, which she ate behind the locked door of her room. At dinner time she'd glare at her mother across the table, & hold forth about health fanatics with atrophied tastebuds.

There were moments when Ramona Bear was sure she saw her daughter grow fatter before her very eyes. She found it painful to see a girl of 13, who measured 5 foot 3, weigh over 200 pounds. For months now she'd been dragging the protesting blimp from diet doctors to therapists. To no avail. Nothing & no one seemed able to distract her daughter from the all-consuming thought of: FOOD.

Ever since her daughter was old enough to sit on a chair, they'd done the egg-standing ritual together twice a year. The last time they'd done it, her daughter had accused her of sadism, making her play with food. & although she'd smiled when her egg stood up, she said: She'd be a lot more thrilled to see it sunny side up, or in an omelette.

& then she'd crushed her egg between her sausage fingers, & slurped down the slimy mess. Telling her mother between slurps how her father had told her that he'd just had to get out, to save his life. How her mother claimed all the space in a room, with her perfect face & perfect figure, until everyone else started to choke. That was why her daughter was making herself huge, to preserve her breathing space.

At that point Ramona Bear had suggested that they should perhaps not live together for a while. That her daughter should perhaps go to a boarding school, or else stay with her father. But her daughter had started screaming that: Her mother wasn't going to get rid of her that easily. She was going to stick around & embarrass her mother, until her mother understood the meaning of embarrassment.

It was true: Her daughter had become an embarrassment to her. It was almost impossible to have friends over   just friends, not even lovers   with an ever-vigilant sentinel in the house. Who'd act pointedly left-out. Or else came on to the friend until he ran out of the house. Her daughter had alienated all her own playmates as well.

I offered my son as a possible companion, worrying how he would react to my fixing-him up with a fat girl, even if the fat girl was maybe an entrance to the fashion world. Ramona Bear sensed my hesitation. She thanked me, but thought we'd be inviting trouble. It might even be the end of our lunches. Which were her oases of sanity in this nuthouse that was her life. & the last thing she wished to give up. Her daughter was a master manipulator.

She rummaged in her handbag, & handed me 3 sheets of paper, covered with minuscule handwriting in brown ink, which her daughter had left lying on the dining room table, for her mother to read & get upset about.

The first one was a poem, retelling the fairytale of Hansel & Gretel. A stylish witch in a forest-green pants suit sticks only Gretel into the rabbit cage. She seduces Hansel who falls completely under her spell, & stuffs his captive sister the way Alsatian peasants stuff geese for gooseliver pate. When Gretel weighs 200 pounds, they smother her with kindness & make an exquisite pate of her liver, which they serve at their wedding reception.
—Ramona Bear was wearing a forest-green pants suit to our lunch that day.

146

The second poem was entitled: THE RAT. An enormous pink rat in a forest-green bathing suit is sitting on a beach under a forest green beach umbrella, surrounded by roasts cheeses breads cakes & a long list of desserts & sweets as far as the eye can see. Its fat aquiver with anticipation, the rat devours everything. Breathlessy with frenzied jaws... / Then eats itself... / Beginning with its paws.

The third piece was called: JUDGE YOUR HONOR, an imaginary dialogue with a tone-deaf mother.

You ask: If I have no self-respect. I don't need to ask: If you have no vanity.

You say that: Shame begins where beauty stops. Let me be your shame then, as I burst into a fashion show with cries of: Mommy...Mommy...

You say that our body is our temple. I say: It's an instrument of perception. If we spend our life adoring the instrument we sure don't perceive very much.

Her daughter must be extremely intelligent: I said in response to Ramona Bear's questioning eyebrows.

She sighed & shook her head: 200 pounds for a 5 foot 3 body wasn't her idea of intelligence, at age 13. Or any age .

That was the last of our lunches. She canceled the next one. & the one after that. Then called to tell me that she was going away for a time, & would let me know as soon as she came back. During the almost 15 years of silence that followed, my son often asked about Ramona Bear. & when I had nothing to tell him, he decided that a prince or a millionaire had carried her off to a castle in Spain.

Suddenly, one evening in March on March 19, to be exact Ramona Bear is on the phone, sounding urgent. Can I come to her house right away, to stand up some eggs & have dinner with her afterwards. She's still at the same stony Upper Westside address. When I hesitate she remembers that I don't like to eat in people's houses, & argues eloquently that: I will have a tremendous variety of food to choose from, all of gourmet quality, catered by La Goulue, where her daughter is the chef. When I accept, she asks that: I wear my black glasses, in a voice that sounds breathless & over-precise with anguish.

I don't know the person who's letting me in. Who vaguely resembles Ramona Bear. A blow-up of the Ramona Bear I remember, hiding under a forest-green tent. I briefly wonder if she may be the over-weight daughter, but the huge face looks too old for a woman of 28.

A woman who speaks with the voice of Ramona Bear, as she sways down the hall ahead of me with the rolling buttocks of a farm horse, & ushers me into a dimly lit dining room, dominated by a long table covered with food. Toward one end, a narrow space has been cleared for 2 raw eggs on a plate. It is only after the enormous creature settles into the chair across from me that I can no longer doubt that this is what has become of the once glorious, perfectly proportioned Ramona Bear. I don't know what to say, & she says nothing either. We stare at our eggs between our hands. They stand very quickly.

Well, that's that: she says, laying her egg back down on the plate: Now we can eat.

I find it hard to swallow, trying not to stare at the feverishly chewing mouth across from me. Into which fat fingers clenched around a fork a knife a spoon rapidly shove chunks of bread topped with all kinds of pate deviled eggs snails prosciutto on melon fish in aspic marinated mushrooms chicken legs duck breast asparagus arugola endives rolled roast beef roast potatoes ham string beans strawberry shortcake raspberry sherbet rhubarb souffle flan cherries flambees. Ramona Bear is aware of my staring at her from behind my black glasses, but she chews away unconcerned.

How's my son? she finally asks during a brief pause. She sounds defiant.

I tell her: My son's fine. He's living on his own now, doing what he always wanted to do: designing clothes. He made the jacket I'm wearing.

Very nice.

I feel her voice hating me. Despising my normal middle-aged silhouette in well-cut clothes.

Her daughter moved out, too. & is very happy working at La Goulue. She'll drop by later. Maybe I can stay & meet her. She makes wonderful food, don't I agree?

The way she says "food" with her lips pursing for suction, turns my stomach. I don't know what to say. I feel that she is trying to provoke me into verbalizing the shock I'm trying to hide. My disgust mixed with anger & contempt at the destruction of what used to be exceptional enviable beauty.

After another long silence, punctured by resumed chewing, she says that: It took her years to work up the courage or the indifference to let me see her again. In case I'd wondered what had become of her. Well, now I knew. But what I didn't know was that she achieved what no overpaid professional doctor therapist psychiatrist specialist in any field achieved: She cured her daughter & her daughter is grateful for it. They're getting along beautifully now.

She had an insight, the day of that last luncheon of ours, almost 15 years ago. Do I remember now she was telling me about her daughter's addiction to food...complaining about her daughter? On her way home she had a realization: Addiction to anything makes you independent from anything but itself. It's like solitary confinement, supplying the company inside your solitary confinement. It's your prison & your refuge. So she thought if she could gain access to her daughter's prison & keep her company, if only for a short while every day, the addiction would lose its autonomy. Perhaps with patience she'd be able to wean her daughter back to a normal shape.

While they're eating their hostile, calorie-conscious dinner that evening, she asks: If her daughter would perhaps like to share the strawberry shortcake she knows her daughter is going to eat in her room by herself after dinner. That way, the strawberry shortcake might provide the social pleasure of shared enjoyment, instead of a shameful private act, committed in hurried secrecy.

Her daughter looks surprised. She thought her mother hated sweets. Desserts.

Yes, well.... Maybe the strawberry shortcake will change her mind.

She almost chokes on the huge piece of cake her daughter piles onto the plate before her. But she forces herself to eat it. Her daughter rapidly eats the rest. Then thanks her mother with a kiss on the cheek.

The next evening they share an apple strudel.

That's how it began. Ramona Bear started to gain weight, & her daughter started to get thinner.

There was a stage, about 9 months into the shared desserts, when her daughter had lost enough to look normal for a 14-year-old. When Ramona Bear still looked plausible. When they were both...pleasantly plump. But when Ramona Bear stopped sharing the desserts, her daughter's weight instantly shot up again. & so Ramona Bear kept eating. The way I'd seen her eat tonight. Now she's no longer able to stop.

She starts to cry then. & I start feeling sorry for her. & afraid for myself, that I, too, might catch the disease of obesity out of compassion for a fat friend. As I stand up, ready to run from the temptation of compassion, her daughter walks in. She's very thin, almost emaciated, with a saintly radiance & a wonderful smile. She's carrying 2 shopping bags which Ramona Bear snatches from her hands. She's no longer crying. She's refilling the platters on the table with pates deviled eggs marinated mushrooms fish in aspic prosciutto on melon.

I ask the radiant daughter: If she drops by like this every night?

Oh yes! she smiles: She couldn't disappoint her mommy. Her mommy is particularly fond of her midnight snack. Why don't I sit down again & help her eat it.

Christal McDougall

Christal McDougall has won several awards for her poetry and was a recipient of a scholarship to the 1993 Aspen Writers Conference and a writing residency at the Ucross Foundation. Her poems have appeared in *The Ledge, Many Mountains Moving, Alligator Juniper,* and the anthology *Details Omitted from the Text: Revisionist Poems on Biblical Women.* She's published fiction in *Women's Work, Alligator Juniper,* and *Sniper Logic.* During the winter, she directs Nordic ski camps for women.

An Ad for Murder

I wish I wouldn't regret throwing things against the wall and listening to them smash—that thud as they hit the wall or the floor and then the shattering of shards across the tile. But there's almost always a sinking dread, trying to pick up the pieces to see if they can be super-glued back together, to see if the spackle matches the color of the drywall in the living room.

Every time I think it will help if I burn her letters at the stove, if I watch her black ink fade as the entire sheet turns dark and ashes off onto the electric burner coil.

And all my friends? They're on her side without even meaning to be. They say, "Be angry, but don't hate her. Think of her as you would think an alcoholic. You wouldn't hate an alcoholic just because he was sick, would you?" It makes sense when they say it. Can't hate mom. Even though she writes that I've been nothing but ungrateful all my life for all I've received. Even though she writes things like:

> Of course your father and I think you are better suited to a program in business. You really should start using that brain of yours! After much discussion, we have decided that if you choose to attend a business school and start exercising that agile mind, we will most happily pay your tuition and expenses. A doctoral degree in business can be a very useful tool! Of course we can't promise the same support

(financial or otherwise) if you choose to
continue your education in another field.
We think you will make the right choice.

And:

Hannah, don't misunderstand us. We
<u>do</u> congratulate you on your present
course in life. We have no doubt that
you can succeed in any pursuit you go
after, particularly if you can overcome your self-centeredness.

I turn the ringer down on my phone, and I sit with the remote
in one hand and a bag of pretzels in the other. I flip through the
only shows that come in: *Gilligan's Island*, *Geraldo*, public TV, news
before noon. Can't believe there are people who do this every day
and that I'm becoming one of them.

My name is Hannah, and I know why I'm here. I'm here
because my parents didn't want an only child. Imagine them
looking at each other across the space between their beds, saying
Honey let's not raise an only child (my sister). *You know how* they *get*.

*She knows I have a system set up in my bedroom for detecting
whether our mother has entered to go through my stuff. We're not allowed
to have locks on our doors because of fire escape rules, so we develop a
secret knocking code and a secret entry code for my room. First she walks
down the hall humming "Three Blind Mice," and then she knocks "Shave
and a Haircut" without the last knock for "cut." I know then that it's my
sister, and I let her in. If I'm not there and she needs to get into my room
she opens the top drawer of my dresser and leaves a hanger in it, hook up.
That way I'll know that if something is different about my room, if there's
a shirt missing or a book out of my shelf, it's because my sister needed to
borrow it and not because my mother was reading my diaries.*

An ad comes on for truck driving school: great benefits, great pay, what a lifestyle for a single woman. An ad comes on for a law firm that specializes in getting you every penny you deserve from your car accident even if it was your fault. An ad comes on for a carpet warehouse, for a paralegal school, for administrative assistant training. An ad comes on for murder.

> Are you tired of receiving harassing phone calls? Are you sick of answering to people who don't understand you and who don't care? Is there someone in your life who you would rather live without? We just might have the answer for you! Send no money! Call now to receive your free brochure! What are you waiting for? Pick up the phone and dial 1-800-2-MURDER, that's 1-800-268-7337. Call now!

I didn't call right away. But I held onto the number in my head for later if I ever decided to use it. You don't forget a number like that.

My name is Hannah and I don't know why I'm here. I don't think I'm like you people. I mean, Ray, I feel for you, I really do. Your wife sounds bad, and I'm sure I wouldn't have handled the situation any differently from you. And Betsy, I'm real sorry for you, too. But I'm not addicted to drugs and I don't smoke except for the occasional joint, and I don't like the way alcohol makes my eyes go squinty, and I don't have AIDS, and I don't think I was molested as a kid, and I'm not pregnant or recovering from anything, really. I wasn't raped or sexually harassed in the workplace or anywhere else. I get the occasional whistle or stare, but it's no big deal. I stare right back and they usually get red and look down at their steering wheel or at the sidewalk.

All I want to know is why I get these letters from my mother.

155

Can any of you help me figure that out? Why do I throw shoes against the wall, and why did I break the ceramic vase that Robert gave me, the one he made? I'm wondering why I stand at the stove and watch her cards and letters blacken before my eyes, why I haven't burned the house down yet, why the smell of singed ink makes me dizzy, why my smoke alarm doesn't go off every time, why I don't tell her to stop writing, why I'm sitting here right now. Why do I sometimes tear her letters up and tape them back together? Why is her file still the fattest one in my file cabinet?

I'm totally serene when I dial the number. I remember when I was a kid, I'd try to make up songs from the different tones on the push-button phone. One was "Camptown Races." When I dial this number I guess I expect it to sound like the theme from Dracula or something, but it doesn't. It sounds like any other number. I let it ring for a while, then I get the creeps and hang up. What the hell am I doing? What if it's really a direct line to the cops?

I sit down for my soap opera. When commercials come on, I switch to another soap on a different channel. I know exactly how long I can watch this secondary soap before I have to switch quickly back to mine. The ad breaks take two minutes, and I keep time on my watch. Today I'm watching a character die. She has cancer, and everyone knows she'll die sometime soon; they're dragging out her painful death for weeks. Maybe they are trying to boost their ratings. Maybe they are negotiating her contract. Maybe she'll renew the contract with the television station and have a miraculous recovery. It's always tough to say. You have to take everything into consideration when you watch soap operas. The story lines are so insipid you can't just buy into them, although tears have welled up in my eyes when I've had a hard day. There are usually one or two really decent actors on the soaps, and once they hire one of those people, the rest of the cast weakens by comparison. The better actors are usually newer characters or younger ones, people who are just breaking into the business. This will be their first stop on a long road of roles before they get into the big time, if they ever do. The older characters are pretty much stuck. They might get a made-for-TV movie if they're lucky, but for the rest of their lives, they'll still be thought of as their soap opera character. They won't be able to be anyone else.

I know why I'm here. My parents wanted a boy. They really thought that since everything else in their lives was so charming and perfect that if they were to conceive another child, it would obviously be a boy, and they could move my sister out of the nursery and totally redesign it just for me (the boy). They'd strip the flowered wallpaper, and they'd paint over the pink floorboards and trim. Carpets and fabrics would be replaced in dark greens and reds, walls would be re-papered in a cowboy motif. Mom would be able to indulge her equestrian fantasies without ever getting mud on her boots.

I'm in the middle of *Gilligan's Island* when the phone rings. I don't pick it up because I'm curious to see who has stolen Mary Ann's coconut-banana pie. The skipper has been waiting for a piece, and the professor's mouth starts watering, too, when he hears about the pie. Of course they think it's Gilligan, who walks in with an empty pie plate, and I'm just wondering how they'll explain where they got the pie plate on a deserted island when Gilligan discovers a second Gilligan, smacking his lips and licking coconut-banana cream off his fingers. I let the machine pick up the call. An ad comes on for 2000 Flushes Toilet Bowl Deodorizer, and I hear my mother's voice on the machine.

"Hannah, it's Mom," she says, then pauses. "If you're there, pick up the phone." I consider letting her think I'm out with my friends or at the store. I glance at the TV, but there are still ads on. This channel almost always runs four minutes of commercials at a time. I grab the phone.

"Hi Mom, sorry. I was washing the bathtub and didn't hear the phone. Hi."

"Maybe you should get a louder ringer, that's what your father and I did. It really helps. He can even hear the phone out in the garage."

"That's OK, Mom. I don't have a garage." I pause to let this sink in. I barely have a house here, is what I'm trying to tell her. "How are you guys?"

"It's your sister, Hannah, that's why I was calling. She'll be going into the hospital next week for surgery. She has cancer..."

Suddenly I see myself on the set of my soap, balanced on the edge of the hospital bed, talking to my sister as if she is the character who is dying, as if she's just an actress playing the role of someone dying of cancer, as if the tears that well up in my eyes are automatic rather than real.

You put the blindfold on, she tells me. I'll take you around the yard. It'll be so cool. You'll have to trust me. Do you trust me? I wrap the bandanna around my head, trying to leave a little space under my eyes so I can at least look at the ground, but when she grabs the ends to tie them under my pony tail, I know it's useless. She pulls the ends tight, ties a big knot back there. This piece of cloth is holding my head together, I pretend. It starts to feel almost secure. If I take this thing off now, I know my head will roll off my neck and down into the grass at the bottom of the field. When we leave the porch, I resist at first, but then I give into it, imagine I'm walking on air; my body is so light without the weight of vision. She tells me exactly where to step, how high to lift one foot and the other. This is where the steps are, she says. You know these steps. Slowly, be careful, do you remember how many there are? I'm thinking as hard as I can: we left the porch and crossed the lawn. We took a right onto the dirt road; I could hear the neighbors' lawn mower; we walked down hill for maybe five minutes. She had me put my hand on the stone wall there at the bottom of the road. We must be at the guest house. Even though I can't see her, I turn toward her. Yes, of course I do! I tell her. We're at the

*guest house. There are five stairs up to the front porch and seven at the
back door. I tell her I think we are at the front porch, and she lets go my
arm so I can climb them myself: one, two, three, four, five. Another step
forward, and I kick the sixth step, and I fall to my knees, and my
hands fly before me to protect my face, and she is suddenly there, on top
of me, pulling at the blindfold, holding me, and she is saying, Hannah, are
you OK? Hannah, I'm sorry, I didn't realize you'd fall, and I'm
yelling at her not to take off the bandanna, it's holding my head on, and
then we're both laughing, rolling on the back stoop of the cottage, and
between gasps, she's still trying to pull my head off, watch it tumble
into the lilacs at the base of the steps.*

In the hospital my sister gets everything she wants. She has
a bed that moves up and down. She has a great remote control. It's
so new and shiny, you can still read the numbers and the labels on
the buttons. My mother has even brought in the VCR from her
family room so my sister can watch movies. She likes to watch old
musicals late at night with the sound really low, but during the day
she'll watch whatever I want to watch. I sit with her for two entire
days before the surgery and then for the week after. I am there for
Good Morning America and I am still there for Letterman. Then
I go home and try to get some sleep. My mother says she doesn't
want me spending the night.

"Give your sister some room to breathe," she says. "She
needs the rest. And so do you." The truth is my mother knows that
I don't need the rest. The truth is that my mother can't stand this.
She hates that my sister would rather spend the days with me than
with her. My mother has pulled me aside in the hall outside my
sister's room and has told me that my sister needs peace and quiet
right now, not the blaring TV set all day and half the night. I have
asked her then why did she feel it was necessary to bring the god
damned VCR if she thinks my sister needs so much fucking rest?
Doesn't she know how hard it is to sleep in a building full of
patients who are coughing and spitting into little troughs at their
necks and who are just about ready to kick off without a moment's

159

notice, these people who are old and sick and rotting away, witnessing their bodies shrink slowly into the folds of their fucking sheets so that one day the nurses come in and instead of changing Mr. Whittaker's bed with him in it, they just assume he checked out of this shit hole in the middle of the night and no one told them? My mother just looks at me in wonderment. "I don't know who you think you are, using language like that in a hospital."

My name is Hannah. I'm here because my sister has cancer and she is right this very minute lying strapped to a bed that moves up and down at the push of a button, and she isn't even wearing the nightie I sent her last Christmas but instead she's got on one of those awful hospital gowns that would make anyone sick, the scratchy way they feel on your ass as you try to use the bedpan or even just roll over to get the crick out of your back. I'm here because I don't want to leave my sister alone with these idiot nurses who talk about her as if she's not there or with my crazy fucking mother who thinks she knows what's best for everyone else and never hesitates to tell you, and who loves my sister more than she loves anyone, looks at my sister with these melty eyes, it's enough to make you throw up. If you saw the way she watches my sister's breathing through the crack in the door you'd swear my sister was an infant in the nursery, just born, just barely holding onto life in the small pink blanket they wrapped around her when she came sliding out of my mother, her skin tinged blue, lips tight shut, quiet as death until they started hitting her, and life and anger began to flow through her veins, and they felt it was finally OK to lay her in the plastic bassinet, the most beautiful, the most fucking perfect face you ever saw, alive and clear beneath layers of plastic so thick you couldn't even feel her breath on your hand.

I know why I'm here. I watch my sister's face as she wakes up from her drug-induced sleep. She's barely able to focus on me at first. Then her lips split into a grin, so slowly, so carefully, it's as if she has to concentrate on each of the twenty-seven muscles that pull her mouth into a smile. Then she speaks. "Get rid of this fucking lunch tray, would you? It's making me sick. And Hannah? Can you get me a Coke?"

I look down at her head on the pillow. "What," I say. "You think the only reason I'm here is to smuggle Cokes into your room?"

"Plus watch TV with me." She reaches for the remote. "You can't watch Oprah by yourself."

I don't do anything except sit with my sister and think about my mother out there in the hallway yakking at nurses and doctors, asking them how long it will be before my sister is released. I've chewed my fingernails down so far they ache. I keep them stuck in a glass of ice water.

We have an electric dryer, but my mother insists we hang the wash on days like this. It's breezy, like there's a storm coming up, and the laundry will dry quickly out here. My sister and I take turns draping towels over the line and straightening them out while the other gets to clip on the clothespins, two per towel, two per sheet, one for each pair of socks and each pair of underpants. Between loads we race around the yard, our energy is high, flying like the wind through the maples and oaks. We dash between the flapping sheets, duck under the hems of skirts and long pants, chase each other in circles around the posts that anchor the clothesline. We are just about to collapse on the grass when my sister looks at me. Let's see how many clothespins it takes to hang you on the line, she says. I'll bet it takes at least 20. I am full of the wind, full of air, feeling so light I bet I can float. OK, I say. I bet it takes 10. From the porch we drag a chair over to the clothesline. Together we stand on the chair, holding tight where we can to each other and to the posts. I wrap my arms around the clothesline so my sister can start hanging me up by the shirt. I wonder how it would feel to have her attach the clothespins to my skin, if she could gather enough between the clip and the line to hold me there, but I keep my mouth shut. She's working slowly, and when she gets to my collar she pauses. We'll

161

have to do something about your head, she says. It's so heavy it might pull you off the line. Stand still while I clip one of these to your hair. I stand still. I hold my head straight up, look across the yard at the neighbors' fence, the roses that poke up over the edge of it. They are beautiful, big, there must be thousands of petals. If I could gather them all and bury my face in them. How they smell. How soft they are. My sister's moving down my other arm, and she's counting. I'm at eleven already, she tells me. No way will you hang by just these. My sister's reaching out from the chair we're on to squeeze on a clip at my left wrist. She's reaching across me, reaching toward that hand, reaching and almost getting there, but the chair is too wobbly, and she pulls it down with her. As she goes she grabs the clothesline to steady herself, and as the chair goes I go too, and all the clothespins pull right off me except the one in my hair. It's happening so fast, the clothesline spins in my sister's hand as she pulls it toward her, my feet land on the ground along with hers, the chair rattles down onto the lawn, and then there's the sudden rebound of the rope, its quick yank away from our fingers, my hair wrapped around it in layers, the sting at the back of my head where the hair doesn't want to separate from flesh. I hold the rope down near my head for 20 minutes while my sister uses scissors on my hair. My mother says she won't pay for a haircut to even up the gap at the back of my neck. She says I shouldn't have been playing in the clothesline in the first place. It takes two weeks for my sister and me to save enough to get the job done.

My father's only partly aware of any of this. My mother has told him what's happening, but I guess he figures this is one area he has no expertise in, hospitals, flowers, get-well and thank you notes. There's nothing he can do, so he stays away. My mother calls him from the phone in my sister's room and tells him he should at least come and visit. "C'mon down here, Honey," my mother croons into the phone. "Hannah's been here every day and I'm sure she could use a break." It's almost nice, how she says it. But I know what's really going on. I know she just wants me out of there.

After lunch my sister and I are watching *Andy Griffith.* It's the one where Barney locks himself in prison because he thinks he's not cut out to be deputy. Gomer tells him in front of a big crowd that he shouldn't pull a U-turn right there in the road, and Barney gets bent out of shape about it and locks himself in a cell. On commercial breaks, I've been flipping through the channels to catch what else is on. I start at the bottom and work my way up as high as these hospital channels go. I stop at one channel because I see something familiar. "...waiting for? Pick up the phone and dial 1-800-2-MURDER. That's 1-800-268-7337. Call now!"

"Did you see that?" I say to my sister. "Can't believe they have this—" I look over at her. Her head's back on the pillow, and her mouth is open. Not wide. Not so wide a fly could go in. Just enough to make breathing easy. She's sleeping so well, I don't even know if she saw them set up a fake robbery so Barney could act as deputy and earn back his good name. I know she hasn't caught the ad for murder. I'm the only one who's seen it.

I'm seventeen the first time I burn something. I'm sick of the thought that my mother's been reading everything I've written for five years or more. I've also started up a false diary that I keep in my bedside table drawer. It even has a key. In it I make up false names for my friends and all sorts of fake incidents that have supposedly happened at school. I write about pretend teachers and once I even drop a hint about a school dance that I set for the second Saturday in December. She gives herself away when she asks me in a pseudo nice tone whether I'll need to go shopping for a dress for the holiday dance. I tell her we don't have a holiday dance at our school. When I think of her looking at my handwriting, I want to kill her.

The pages come out of my fake diary pretty easily, and I stand at the stove in my mother's kitchen and watch them burn. I like to see the burner coils singe through the paper in rings before a flame flares up. My mother and father are out for the evening the first time I do this, and when they ask me why the house smells like smoke, I just say I wanted to light a fire and I didn't realize the flue was closed. I hear them in the kitchen later. That girl is so strange, my mother says. I don't know what goes through her head. Sometimes I think she's not even our daughter.

The day my sister gets released from the hospital my mother's running around like she's insane. She's so excited she can't sit still. My sister's told her to calm down, she's bothering the other patients, but my mother isn't listening. She's busy telling the nurses that my sister is finally going home where she'll get the kind of care she needs and deserves, the kind of love and attention a person in her state of mind can really use at a time like this.

"Nothing like a little TLC from her mother," my mother says. "That'll bring her around. You just wait and see. No more of this up-and-down bed, this TV all hours of the night. No more of that." My mother is puffed up like a hen now. I hate to think of her getting her hands onto my sister, treating her like fragile china.

As my mother darts around the hospital room packing my sister's things—looking at each of them tenderly, as if every item of clothing, the clock, a few books, some flower arrangements, a special pillow, as if each of these things has become my sister in some way—she gives me orders. "Hannah," she says. "I don't want you calling every day. Your sister needs some peace and quiet. She needs some rest. You need rest too, Hannah. Your sister will not be bored at the house, she'll be getting the kind of rest she needs, and I don't want you bothering her. I expect that you'll respect that and let her recover in peace."

I want to tell her that I do need rest, she's right, I need rest from her voice telling me how wonderful and perfect my sister is, how delicate and lovely, how we all have to treat her very carefully or she might crash suddenly to the floor and shatter. I want to say, What about me? What about the kind of rest I need? How about some peace for me? How about leaving me alone for a week so I don't have to hear your voice or see your curlicued hand writing every time something goes wrong. How about buying me a gas stove so that I can burn your letters with real flame instead of just heat that singes through too slowly before it catches the flame. It happens so slowly, I almost have time to regret it, and I don't want to regret anything. I want to take an entire manila folder full of your writing and watch the flames eat away at the ink, pull the center from its edges, compare how stationery burns with how plain paper burns. There's got to be a difference.

Hannah, this is really really important, my sister says. We're sitting on the steps of the school. It's late in the day; most of the practicing teams have wrapped up their drills or scrimmages and have headed for the showers. My sister's voice is heavy, and I turn my head to look at her. She is staring across the lawn at the flagpole, the 7-Eleven, the kid walking his dog across the street. I haven't had a period for 75 days, she tells me. What am I gonna do if? Tad will kill me. She's looking at her feet now, picking at a toenail. I don't even want to think about Mom and Dad, she says. I don't want to think about them either. Seems like this isn't any of their business, like it's just one more thing my sister and I have to deal with together. I know my words won't make things OK, so I put my arm around her shoulders. I don't know, I tell her. We'll think of something.

A couple days later my mother calls me downstairs. I can't imagine what she wants, so I'm not worried. My grades are good, I'm not in trouble at school. I get down there and she's got my diary in her hand. I want to throw up. I know what it is. I've written in there about my sister thinking she's pregnant, and my mother's seen it. She believes everything she reads in that fake diary, and I can see she believes this, too. What do you think you're doing, writing about things like this in here, she says. What kind of a person writes this about her own sister? How dare you commit this to paper and say absolutely nothing to me? Don't you think a mother has the right to know about this? She's going on and on; I can barely keep up with the stream of reprimands.

This is the moment I have to decide. Do I tell her everything that's happening, or do I tell her I've been making up stuff all along and let her think this is just another story? I stand with my back to the refrigerator. I can't decide. No words are coming out of my mouth. After three solid minutes of silence, my mother throws up her hands. My fake diary is on the table in front of her. You think I'm not onto you? she says. You think I don't know you're out to ruin your sister?

I know the number by heart, and I dial it with a pencil eraser so there are no fingerprints on the push buttons of the phone. Someone answers. He asks my name, the address for service, how I intend to pay. I tell them I'll meet them there and pay C.O.D. We set the time. I feel a big lump in my throat, but I keep breathing, I keep breathing.

I imagine what'll happen when they arrive. I'll be waiting, the cash in my pocket curled in a tight fist. The guy will come in. He'll look like the Orkin man, the Terminator, one of the Ghostbusters. He'll be wearing a space suit and carrying a big box with a gun attached to the end of it, as if he'll stand at the bottom of the stairs and let out a big blast. Everyone in the house will slowly fall asleep like the bugs under the refrigerator. Later he'll come and sweep us all up.

Or he'll look like a doctor paying a house call. His white jacket will hang loosely over his blue oxford cloth shirt. Pens will stick out of a breast pocket. He'll be carrying a briefcase in which I imagine an entire assortment of needles and different drugs, special formulas developed for individual cases. He's taken the time to concoct a formula especially for this job. He'll have a tight schedule: "Got another appointment in half an hour, let's make this quick."

I want it to be quick, too. I'm tired of having things happen so slowly. I'm tired of having to wait for the flame to catch on my mother's letters. I'm tired of sitting through commercials, of waiting for my sister to get better, of waking up in the night, of being told what I may and may not do, of the headaches that ride at the back of my neck. Yes, I want it to be quick and painless. I don't want to have to say goodbye. I don't want time to regret anything.

Lucy Hochman

Lucy Hochman's fiction has appeared in *The North American Review*, *The Iowa Review*, *Transgressions: The Iowa Anthology of Innovative Fiction*, *The Village Literary Supplement*, and *Caliban*. She lives in rural North Carolina and makes contemporary quilts from found fabric and other objects.

The Imaginary Wars of Bellford County

In Bellford County, whole banks and acres of shore are covered with bubbles and beetle-sized hermit crabs, grabbing and swapping. There is a common belief around here, a custom or the belief of a custom, that what children are doing when they dig holes, and children will dig holes if offered some dirt or find themselves on the beach, is digging a hole to China. Have they heard of China? Do they want to be elsewhere? They like the feel of grit on their hands, the way the earth changes temperature, how sometimes water suddenly seeps into the place they've created for it as if it had been waiting for the right moment. Maybe they like being able to make the thing they so routinely stand upon change shape; it goes down where it hasn't before. For now, we'll set aside the way they build a pile at the same time, the way they create an illustration of opposites. In Bellford County, people try to make sense of the way their neighbors behave. They look around, gathering evidence from their surroundings, constructing relationships between disperate elements of their experiences, constructing plains in their minds on which the possibilities they invent do a form of dance, or conversation, or battle. Colloquially, they say they're thinking.

For instance, all along the bubbling shores, hermit crabs were grabbing and swapping, and farther up the beach, past the dunes and on the edge of the city, Professors George and Lila had been married twenty years. Lila was forty and George was fifty when George and Lila's best friend Marian began speaking

German to each other during faculty dinner parties at George and Lila's lovely home, and Lila would become uncomfortable, and take a bottle to the finished garden shed she used as an office, drink the darn thing. and then return to the house where they were playing James Brown records. Lila, easily the youngest and prettiest of the professors, could shake her tail like nothing else, and back inside, in the haze, the German babbling sounded like distant elephant calls, and elephants can communicate over miles, and crocodiles bellow when they hear a low B flat, and sometime later, Lila moved out of the house with the garden she'd cultivated while George sat by the pool with his beer and favorite students, and this time Marian moved in, and graded her papers in the finished shed, and bellowed in German from the little window towards the pool, "Hey, George, lemme have one of those beers!" and Lila still had to see them at work, because they were all in the same department, so Lila started hanging out with physics people, though she understood their concepts only as metaphors.

Lila thought, people must be interchangeable, arranging themselves around the common stalk of their community.

When news of the split-up dribbled to gossip, imaginary court cases ensued. Many students had been impressed with George, and many had been impressed with Lila, and they wanted someone to be at fault, so they could decide with whom they might want to take more classes.

There's an ocean floor, and along it live creatures bound by large, exaggerated parts of their anatomy. Everyone could see the crabs, but there, farther into the water lived these various forms of moss animals, called Bryozoa.

The Bryozoa are composed of thousands of nearly microscopic individuals called zooids which are embedded in the rind of a flexible common skeleton, such that the structure looks like a budding sapling. When the colony is in seawater and left undisturbed, the zooids unfurl a minute funnel-like crown of tentacles, and filter-feed by pumping seawater and suspended particles through their tentacles. The water and what's going on in it tell the colony what to do.

Or each zooid is enclosed in its own box-like exoskeleton and the upper surface of the colony is covered with a flexible membrane. Muscles attach to the inner surface of this membrane, and control the feeding tentacles of the zooids, which pop out when the great muscle contracts.

Or the body, which is called the calyx, is white and cup-like. It rests on a long, muscular stalk. Up to twenty-five short ciliated tentacles project from the cup into the water. The base of the stalk enlarges to a muscular bulb and forms a flexible joint with the creeping rootlike stolon. The stolon interjoins all members of the colony. The stalks of living individuals sway, bend, nod, and twist. When an individual is disturbed, the stalk bends rapidly and presses the individual against the substratum, perhaps to avoid predation. Calyxes are sometimes lost or discarded, leaving only a naked stalk. The stalks regenerate the missing calyx.

Some people in Bellford County thought of Lila and then of Bryozoa, and some of those people took one series of facts and used it to make sense of the other. Some people did not think of Bryozoa at all. Some people did not know Bryozoa existed, and some had never heard of Lila. They kept busy thinking about other aspects of Bellford County, and as they related one series of facts to another, bits of evidence came into conflict, and people found themselves resorting to notions of opposites which were built into their society, and, it seemed, into the language itself. They found themselves constructing imaginary court cases in an effort to make decisions about what they'd witnessed first hand or by virtue of hearsay. They found themselves unable to make do with what they knew.

For instance, some people noticed that occasionally, one woman or another stood alone on the beach and gazed, with longing, at the ocean. Driving along the stone wall which separated the dunes from the highway, people saw a woman standing with a hand to her brow, and thought they could see her whole life from the pose she struck. They thought they could see her particular life as well as the sort of life they imagined she represented.

She stood in a blue-green dress, one cut on the bias. The fabric had blue strands running one way and green strands running the other, so that when it blew in the wind, it seemed to flash blue to green, with the waves which were crosshatched with wind, though the waves flashed with more grayish tones. She'd parked on the highway's shoulder, and her car was cluttered with things her Lovingman had shoplifted and forgotten, from when in good times they'd romped, full of disdain, through the city. Somewhere he stood or wafted, feeling terribly occupied with his feelings.

How he moved her here and there, from lush jungles to deserts with sand and the smell of armpits, leisurely or else with gumption, in a clamoring rush, piled high with passion, or in a U-Haul, or graciously, or one quiver at a time, as a snail moves, adulating the ground it covers with mucus, and indeed, from her cockles to her muscles, to tears and with warbles. How he moved her from side to side, across the plains, consorting with the adulation and the undulation, as one moment to the next he erased her days with the desperation he evoked and from which he sidled. There she gazed in retrospect at the water that rubbed itself. No, no, she cried like an ocean bird, I am the captain, I am the one lost at sea.

She stole, she was a liar, or people didn't know what to believe, knowing only that they didn't want to believe her, in her shiny billowing gown, as she conjured an historical army of shore women and their emotional straits. Occasionally a person recognized in himself a desire to feel sorry, but squelched the impulse, perhaps not knowing if sorrow was an ethical response to her despondency, which might have implications of vagrancy and a lack of respect for the status of community.

People thought what a figure she cut, mourning, adding her

tears to the salty sea, conjuring the whole tired history of losses and love lost. Commonly, they felt she'd been fed her just deserts: "desert" as in what is deserved, and "desert" the place that balances the sea (not kind to the tongue). But "dessert," the one with the double letter, because you want another, they refused to recognize because it rocked the other two connotations. They could not remember at what point, in the history of the phrase, word play had begun. In the imagined court cases which ensued, the meanings of these words came up and into conflict, and everyone had his say and his day in the sun. She was a distraction. She blocked up the view. Her silhouette on the horizon formed a rift in the sky. People ground their teeth, as if they waited for him, too, and wondered, do we mourn for her or against her, as she stands, busy crabs covering her feet, and cuts a figure in the wind? Everyone knows she won't see him again.

Elsewhere, avoiding predation, Lovingman also moved himself. He was never to see her again. He hadn't gone to sea at all. He'd stolen a car and gone off with things she'd stolen. It was her privilege to think of love as a crutch, to hack off a limb so she'd have something to mourn, to crave the attentions of passersby, the desire in truth for a homecooked pie or a bed in someone's backyard shed, thinking No, no, I want to be the one lost at sea, tugging sails, singing, bailing, riding the crow's nest, pointing at whales, coiling ropes and gnawing dried blubber, too busy to complain, too full of the sea and the way it moves, and the way one moves in it.

People wanted to prosecute someone for shoplifting, because the rest of the story left them uncertain of what to say, because they became confused about which aspects of their reflections were actually memories of what they'd witnessed and which aspects they'd imagined, and which, of the various combinations, were actually relevant to which of the possibly implied cases at hand. What can you do when you can't decide? Let her writhe on the beach for her thieving lover.

In Bellford County there were beaches, mountains, cities, even deserts, but somewhere in its forgotton history, when the maps were hand-drawn and people knew of little past their shoes, for a long period of time, the hermit crabs had ranged far inland along the streams which fed the estuary, and foxes had traveled from the forest to gobble the prone bodies as they slithered from shell to shell. A community of people had abandoned the place because the mosquitoes were so bad and their houses kept sinking into the marsh. They'd kept manic records of their failed crops and carved their mortality rates into the trunks of big old trees, but a hurricane tore the forest down.

In the center of Main City in Bellford County was a great mirrored complex which took up a whole block, and parts of it bridged the highway. There were six towers filled with stores and more were growing. Magpies were naturally attracted to the city. They never learned that if you dive for the sparkles—and there are so many, the sun makes them on the glass and on the chrome of cars, isolated bursts of light—if you dive for one, it will disappear, and in the moment you realize it isn't there and are looking for where it has gone, you will crash into the building or a car will crash into you. Brothers and sisters of them, droves of them spotted, dove, and died. They could drive themselves to extinction that way, killing themselves for what was a matter of perspective and proximity.

In a great glass box of an apartment building lived a man with abbreviated fingers who was just beginning to recognize the connection between his self-destructive practices and the sexual desire he felt for his sister. The night before, he'd been drunk, dropping lengths of dental floss into her toilet as he flushed it, remembering how his fingers got the way they were, how when he was eleven Caroline had refused to let him into the bathroom while she was showering and he'd run into his room and stared at his industrial-strength fan, taken the cage from the front and stuck his hand into it. Dizzy from the memory of the fan and the still-flushing toilet, he'd rushed into the living room, turned off the record player, and announced to the roomful of dancing office cohorts, "Caroline and I are going to the park now, to relive our childhood and push each other on the merry-go-round, and you can all go home," but they didn't.

He leaned out his window and searched for his reflection in the glass across the street. On a whim, he took a coin from his penny loafers (it was a dime for extra luck,) and flicked it into the street. It flashed where it landed and immediately a black bird dove toward it and slammed into a signpost, which made sense.

The abbreviation of the lives of the birds, the act of looking into many mirrors at once, the dizzying effect of the facts on a particular man's life, these aspects, when called up and into conflict, upset the citizens of Bellford County. They wanted to decide which metaphor created an answer. They wanted to set the metaphors against one another and watch them duke it out.

The aspen forests on the mountain of Bellford County were filled with wildflowers and spotted with meadows. A family went on a picnic there, and the child wandered into the trees with the dog. Together, they dug holes. The child said "dig," and pointed to the ground, and the dog dug a hole. Then the child took the pile of dirt and tried to press it into the shape of an arch, like the causeway she'd seen on the way out of Main City to the beach. This dirt behaved no better than the sand had, and collapsed into a mound which looked like the hole, but inverted.

Amidst the imaginary court cases which ensued, as people were humming and drumming out the evidence to themselves, a woman remembered to herself like so:

A man came into my house, convinced me we used to be lovers, and took a bunch of my stuff. It isn't interesting how he convinced me; he convinced me, he did it, I believe him, I'd believe anybody, it seems true.

"He was crawling in through the window, but I wasn't alarmed, because he looked so familiar with all he had—all the fingers, the dark outfit, and the two legs and two arms and two eyes, ears, and nostrils. Also, his shirt was tight enough that I could tell a navel lay beneath and could almost see the hairs around it, recognized instinctively that they'd be glossy and winding. If he'd had a cape, perhaps then I'd have wondered, but all that showed was recognizable. It's true, I've fucked many things which show through some fabrics, I've licked elbows and armpits and all were present in the man from the window. I believe he was as much my ex-lover as any of my ex-lovers. Now everyone wants me to question my empty house, but I recognize it as mine as well as when it was full, though it has been other people's. Besides, I owe, I know.

"Here, I'll help you, I said, as is my nature, tell me where to put it, would you like a good liquid drink, I'll make it stiff, how symmetrical you are, as usual, and how good of you to come by and give focus to my evening."

Past the beach, and inland from Main City, lived the forest of aspen. The landscape, for a while, can be seen as a series of vertical lines, as one follows the regular trunks of the aspen and notes the silk, taupe dignity of the skinlike bark, and rides with the comfort of their regularity. Then the eyes dart from one unrealized branch bud to the next—another regularity, one of dots on a grid—and then reach the coin-sized leaves, and these are in motion, clacking and flashing, recalling the tone of the trunk, while putting that pattern in its place among others, because one hasn't yet considered the cedars or the clean ground of ferns, grass and purple flowers, or the small pond or path as a point of reference. Each aspect goes along repeating, and each merges with another before it might seem complete.

The aspen forest, it has been proven, is built like a castle with many turrets, like strawberries, and like moss creatures. These individuals are linked underground, somewhere there is a center or a source or a beginning though no one can tell where it is, and the trees stretch, genetically identical, and are anomalized by weather, by the moments through which they have stretched. In it, a woman has just given birth to quintuplets. She's a tough forest girl, has been denied an education and lives within the bark of her ignorance, didn't know why her belly was so much bigger than other girls' had been, didn't know she ought to be at a hospital. It wasn't like she was sick after all, but she expected to die of it. So she sent her sister for the harried midwife, went on about the business of birthing, and there they were, partially mangled, two of them that had needed their feet cut apart from each other, but stitched up, lain out and screaming like any room full of babies.

Her common-law husband made his way from work to the shack, walking the mile through the aspen from where he can park his car. The sky was a carnival of masks and the mud he crossed frozen in topographical mountains from deer tracks and streams which operate only in springtime. By the time he got home the babies were nursing or sleeping.

In the imaginary court case which ensued, the girl who gave birth is on the stand, glancing from one oak bench to another at the citizens in their defining, limiting, and, it seemed to her, lying costumes. "I am a judge," or, "I set the record straight," or, "I am your peer," the costumes said, the people they enclosed desperate to feel sure of something. The girl tries to explain why one of the babies that had its heels born attached to a sister ended up dying after all.

"He pulled her head out by the roots," she says, of her husband. "He held it under his arm, upsidedown, and stirred it with a stick like a bowl of batter." How come? "He looked at those feet and looked at his own. Couldn't see the connection."

Internal contoveries raged. People wondered: Who preys on whom? Who is ever the real deserter? They thought of exposed bodies leaping from outgrown homes, and wanted to shake one

177

another by the shoulders and cry: what do you mean outgrown? Where does the individual stop and the community begin? When is a life anything but abbreviated? How is it possible to be convinced despite the evidence? At what point, with a clear conscience, can you shrug at the evidence and bow out? And for God's sake, will the real metaphor please stand up?

In Bellford County there were beaches, mountains, cities, bogs, and deserts, and in a way there were rainforests, bluffs, prairies, canyons, moors, volcanic fields, and starry space. Amidst the landscapes, a mother watched her child digging holes and piles. At first, the child giggled when the dirt resisted, clinging to itself or slipping from the constructed peak into the little well. Soon, the child became frustrated as the towers crumbled and the banks of the hole collapsed. The mother watched her baby's features grow tense, and redden, and in an effort to keep him from actually crying, she scooped him up and carried him away. Terrified for him and astonished at her terror—digging holes is a custom, after all—she thought: what is it in a child that is born to distort? "Honey, leave it alone," she whispered in his ear, "Believing in what you invent can kill you."

The imaginary court cases in Bellford County were beginning to distract people from their chores. One young man noticed that many of his school chums were getting personally involved: some were married or divorcing, having children, building houses that were bound to get washed away by the ocean or shaken to bits or torn apart by an earthquake, hurricane, or tornado, trying to build bridges between the rich and the poor, rehabilitating or arresting addicts, cultivating community gardens, buying boats so they could catch or sell fish and those were just the ones who'd stayed near Main City. Others had gone to Washington, Chile, or Prague.

The young man remembered a war his father told him about, how he'd been shipped overseas to settle a dispute, and how a great many people had died. It occurred to the boy that war is a court case, plus lots of death; references to the absolutes as good as nods from the head of a marionette.

But what had really affected the young man, as a boy hearing about war— secondhand to be sure— was that the city his father bombed was also the home of a zoo, where there were lots of animals in cages. His father had walked through the zoo, and there were charred and infected animals in their cages, giraffes who'd broken their necks trying to plunge through the bars, gorillas wheezing and dying of smoke inhalation, burnt birds, crocodiles and turtles belly up in water covered with oil that had fallen from the sky.

It was an arduous task, but the boy planned and planned, and then one night he let all the animals at the Main City zoo out of their yards and cages. The animals ran around the mirrored complex, along the beach, and into the forest. They died exotic deaths, eating the wrong each other, infecting themselves with unfamiliar parasites while trying to cross the sidewalk from one continent to another. Giant parrots fell from the sky, their bodies having spanned the telephone wires they perched upon; wolves broke into people's houses, ate defrosting chicken from people's countertops and got salmonella; aardvarks drank from chlorinated fountains; camels electrocuted themselves on subway tracks; gazelles broke their knees on pavement; goats slid off draw-bridges and fell into the estuary.

They didn't know it, but amidst the imaginary court cases which ensued, people's thoughts were arguing. The portly prosecution snorkeled around in the ocean and said, "There is a war," and the thin defense tried on shoes at the glass mall and said, "There is no war." Prosecution pointed to the rampant abstraction of situations into pros and cons and issues of fault. Defense said "Yes, as always, people are unable to consider more than they are able to consider." Prosecution put the garbage on the curb, saying "It's like when you're digging a hole— the more you do, the more stuff you don't know what to do with" and defense clipped away at a child's hair, saying, "Well, you can't have a hole without taking a bunch of dirt out."

"But on the other hand you can't have a pile of dirt without digging yourself a hole."

"But on the other hand it's more like hermit crabs. At first you think you're getting bigger and better. Then you realize you just don't want to get caught with your pants down."

"But on the other hand, it's not that simple. We're interdependent but we're too small to recognize our common source."

"Like trying to compare yourself to the ocean."

"Don't change the subject."

"I'm not— I'm saying there may be holes and crabs and so on, but we're all magpies anyway, destroying ourselves for irrational notions of beauty."

"You have no idea what it's like to be a magpie."

"I'm agreeing with you."

"You're not. You're the fellow in the forest of aspen who thinks there are a bunch of trees."

"You think I can't see the forest for the trees? You think I can't hear them falling?"

"No, I think you can't see your feet because your belly's too big. I mean you can't see where you're going because of where you've been."

They noticed that some mannequins don't have ears but still have earrings, and that a mouse doesn't say "bad hawk"— a mouse just hopes the hawk will go away. They decided you can't hate poor people because they don't have enough money, and that whether you're trying to lose something or trying to find it, you never know whether to stand still or move around. Besides, they thought, opposites attract. All admissible evidence having been cited, witnesses excused, the name of justice raised and upheld, and regardless of the grievances set before the presupposed criteria aforementioned, in that in reference to restitution and begged indulgences someone wanted to rest, someone said:

"We're comparing apples and oranges here."

And someone responded:

"Well, it takes two to tango."

"Well, it takes one to know one."

"You don't know what you're saying."

"I can lead you to water but I can't make you drink," said someone.

"Time will tell," someone said.

"One day at a time."

"It's like living in a zoo, trapped because freedom will kill you."

"Life goes on," someone said.

"But your just deserts are just dessert."

"And a language less arbitrary would be inaccurate."

It was true. Fog, night, air, time, beetles, and babies crept over Bellford County. The glass walls in Main City repelled or absorbed light, and blended or contrasted with the sky. The trees grew up and down; the water lapped the shore and went out to sea. People quit but went on. No one knew what they were thinking.

Lidia Yuknavitch

Lidia Yuknavitch writesfucksdrinksachesteachers in Oregon. She is drivenmadhungrytiredbisneaky. She is the managing editor of the irreverant *two girls review*. Her work has appeared in *Postmodern Culture*, *Left Bank*, *The Northwest Review*, *Critical Matrix*, *The Rain City Review*, *Quarry West*, *ART:MAG*, and other fancy-pants journals. Her forthcoming short story collection is *Her Other Mouth*.

from *Loving dora*

*I am aware that—in this town, at
least—there are many physicians
who (revolting though it may seem)
choose to read a case history of
this kind not as a contribution to
the psychopathology of neuroses,
but a "roman à clef" designed for
their private delectation.*
—*Sigmund Freud, 1905*

MY OWN CASE HISTORY

mother is cleaning the spoons again and there is just no other
way to say this…the spoons, shining their convex concave wickedness reflect back at her the only image she could ever be.
Elongated head, eyes so long they scoop away at the rest of the
face. The rubbing and rubbing the outside curve, the flipping
over and violent rubbing again in the dip of the poor, silvery
utensil.

I can see the inside out of this city, the gray to blue to black
like the bruise on a thigh, the streets running for all they're worth
like tracks, the pedestrians fading from color to black and white
in sheets of almost rain. She's got me sitting at this little card table
next to the window. She's got me in this silky nightgown and terry
robe. The patterns of wet make sight Vaseline over. What a lump
of drooling illness. Illness is the most useful form of love. How
right I am next to this window bleeding its window life over and
over against the dumb outside. Maybe I am the organs of this city,
maybe I am the pink terry heart and lungs, maybe I am the red and

183

swollen reproductive organs of this whole stupid colorless world. I am secreting, I am dead and reproducing. She will clean the spoons until she wipes herself into silvery, shining, cupping, nothing.

hysteria is an occasion for sexual excitement, so they say. But what else is sixteen but pure excess? I prefer to spend my time looking at Francis Bacon Paintings and thinking about inside jokes between me, Sylvia Plath, and Anne Sexton. I mean, you want to live life on the edge, right? You want to take the order of things and abandon it, replace it with pain and risk. That is what it is like for me at sixteen. I am just doing what comes natural. You pierce your nose, you shoot up, you read the old guys—burroughs and de sade and rimbaud and bataille and artaud (my dad keeps giving me Jim Morrison books…it's like reading cartoons) you dive into music that throbs you out of your stupid body so you can breathe in the heat and sweat of anyone but you. You let go, see, you let go of the death grip of life and dive into the not you, the not me, the slamming and pounding and screaming of your pulse and your blood into a hundred thousand others. Every generation is lost, not because of a generation gap, but because of a different gap: they had history, we don't. We have TV. Me and all my friends would kill all the TV's in Seattle if we could. We ritually kill them at The Den routinely.

When he first came on to me, Mr. K, the friend of my father's, he had a butter knife in his left hand. Who knows why a butter knife, he just did. Just me and him in the living room. Just rain whispering like nuns against the pressure of the walls. He had this butter knife in his hand, accidentally, and he crossed the carpet to me, he was trembling, he put his hand on my thigh, he put his other hand near my collar bone, and the cold silver rested against my skin. He bit me on the neck and he whimpered. It was like something out of a Lon Chaney movie. It was like I was in some archaic, alien world. What in the world did he think he was doing? I pulled out my pocket-knife. I flipped open the blade. He took a step back, thinking it was for him, I guess. I held the tiny, useless blade in the air between us. I drew the blade to my own collarbone, to the very place he had trembled. I slit the skin open in a red, thin, perfect, smile.

That was the beginning between me and Mr. K, I guess. It's not so bad. It keeps the house in order.

The Den is packed every single night. I've been coming here for years. Sometimes I ache so hard waiting for the windows of the apartment to blacken into night that I can burst a blood vessel in my eye. I mean I can stare that hard. The people at The Den are my family. Cutters, junkies, and sadists are loved for who and what they are. Talk about unconditional love. All I remember about the first night I ever showed up there was that Greta led me with her hairy hand down the back stairs and into the back room of the place. She had the calves of a line-backer and the seams up the back of the hose looked ready to split. I swear the walls were pulsing in that room because on the other side was my dream world. Greta said, hey everybody, this is dora. And she lifted up my shirt and my beautiful scars shone like white bone lace around my ribs and belly. Then we went out into the club and my whole life was born into itself, my whole fucking life gave over into tears of joy and longing. Some people take their whole lives to find home.

objects for barter keeps running through my brain like a ticker tape right across my forehead. I hear a little clicking noise too when I see it. The clicking of age typing itself over the bodies of babies. It's all so transparent. My father doesn't want my mother to know that he has been balling Mrs. K for two years. He tells Mrs. K "it's like ice, it's like a steel rail up your spine and the cold and lonely of a corpse-woman." He thinks mother doesn't know; it's the most fucked up scenario in the whole world. Mother brushes her hair in front of her vanity at night. Instead of the tubes and boxes and brushes meant to paint a face alive on a woman, small brown bottles, white bottles, little bitty bottles with lines and lines of instructions point up at her, draw her down to them like blush and perfume ought to draw down the face of a woman.

185

The more she knows the more she doesn't know.

If I was a painter I would paint her face like that, melted with sedation and the ups and downs of a mother never meant to mother.

He talks right over my knowing too, I start with a little "a-hem" here and there, a little "I've got a tickle in my throat" when he talks about the K's coming to stay with us because of his own failing health, because Mrs. K is a good caretaker, a trained nurse, because we have all been friends for years. I start really wolfing them out though, I start coughing up phlegm and hacking away, drowning him out like I am choking on something, and get this— he just talks louder and louder, or sometimes, lately, he leaves the room as if he has just remembered something urgent. If I wanted to, I could cough loud enough to shatter the walls like shells, I could explode every cage of ribs in the house. My voice is more and more hoarse from all the coughing.

Like most things in this life, it's about economy, it's about a fair deal that everyone can live with. The K's come to stay and attend to Father's health. Father sends daughter to shrink so that she can have the carnal knowledge sucked out of a tiny hole in her skull. Shrink agrees as a favor to a friend to get his daughter to stop coughing and fainting publicly at inopportune moments. Mother cleans and cleans those little spoons. Someday she will wear the heads right off of them. A family cannot live with itself. There must be a story to house it, to sleep with it, to spoon the medicine into the mouth and tuck it in at night. Daughter tells shrink everything about everyone until he is positively titillated. After all, she's seen her go down on him, and she's seen her father's mouth to the mouth of her, and she has a very good eye for detail, and she knows if she keeps telling the story of her tragic home life then the shrink will never touch her inside or out, he will never read the Braille of her flesh, he will never trace the tracks home, he will never take her mother-loving life away from her, he will never kill her worlds.

She says, "yeah, I dream. Who doesn't?"

Right before a night out is the best. Tonight it's The Cure more deafening than the roar of youth. She sits in front of the mirror and pulls her platinum hair back with a band. She draws a thick black at each eyebrow. She draws a blacker than black streak underneath the tiny lashes cradling her blue eyes. She lets the lips bleed into the cut of cherry red, like a gash at the mouth. She takes her shirt off. The black and blue lace of tonight carries her small breasts like precious fruits into the night. Before she climbs into her black leather jacket and out the window and down the fire escape, she puts the tube, the needle, the spoon in her inside pocket, because if she waits until she gets there she will be drooling with wait, she will be aching in every vein, screaming through every want in her body, and everybody can do it together. The best.

j'apelle un chat un chat, the fucking funniest thing she has ever heard in her life. He said it and she burst out laughing so loud it wasn't even a laugh, it was too cacophonous, to much for her little girl-body. J'apelle un chat un chat. Do you masturbate. He was explaining himself. He was not afraid to call a spade a spade. He was speaking to her respectfully, like an adult. He then went on to describe for her that the fantasy material of the masturbation scene could tell us a lot about the repressed desire or anger of the individual, like dreams, the fantasy is built out of what the psyche considers dangerous material. He was explaining all this to her and she was daydreaming about The Den, about how far and away they'd all gotten from these ideas, about how she wasn't even sure this guy knew he had a body. So she told him, "yeah, I masturbate. Doesn't everyone?" She wanted to know what he would think if he was strapped-in to the pleasure throne at The Den and all the tongues and cocks and mouths were dripping and sucking and licking at him, would his glasses fall to the floor and smash his sight forever from his eyes, would the cat-o'-nine-tails, when it came down on his belly, his genitals, leave him screaming or silent, would he cough? Honestly, she thought this was the funniest fifty minutes of her long and happy life. "Uh-huh, I just picture me and Mrs. K licking each other and my father can't quite get into the room because his cock is so enormous that it doesn't fit in the door, you know, like in those Aubrey Beardsley prints, and he is so horny he is breaking down, he is really losing it, he is unbearably and violently holding himself, unsure of whether or not his huge coming will kill him." Next visit he's going to talk to me about the danger of AIDS, I bet. As if any of us even think about sex anymore. As if we haven't already had five years of French, Bushmill's whiskey, a needle in the arm and death by sex all around us before we are sixteen.

coughing up silence because there really isn't any good reason to cough anymore, he can see that the shrink is a lot more interested in what I am telling him than in saving his butt, he doesn't even want me to go anymore, says he won't put up with it, he won't pay for it. Mr. K goes in me and it's just so dumb to think that a man could really believe in his own member anymore. None of the men I know do. Who are these men that they think they can live centuries back? I'm not coughing anymore but some nights I dream I crawl into bed with Mrs. K. Everyone has separate rooms now but some are joined by doors and others are not. She lets the crouch of dreams crawl out of my fingers between the folds of flesh. She lets me tongue her nipples by feigning sleep or love. Maybe it's because she's tired of being made love to like Emma Bovary, maybe she always wanted a daughter, maybe she's just glad someone can get it right without your having to tell them a thing. Maybe she understands the hands of a child.

visiting the dead, that's what the relief of going to The Den is like for me a sixteen year old girl. The men I know are dying—either literally or with desire for all the other men in the world. I love them all as if they brought me into the world, I want to daughter over all their grief. I love Greta and Greta is dying for Michael, and I love Michael too, Michael the archangel, sweet boy unafraid to be a man. And I love a girl named Obsidian. She's Algerian. I want to bring her home but who wants to show anyone the dreaded oedipal family dragging their arms and legs and half-

dead members around like crab-claws? I want to put her in pillows
and rose petals and oil and prop her up and then I want to cut for
her, just under the ribs, my most intimate spot, like jesus. I want
to draw the blade across the white scar-over-scars slow as a secret
and I want the deep red to drip open to her, only to her.

Before father stopped paying him, I told him the first dream,
and he said that I was afraid of Mr. K raping me, but that I was even
more afraid of myself, my own desire for Mr. K. When I told him
the second dream, he said I had killed father in the dream because
Mrs. K was the strongest unconscious current in my mental life,
she was, after all, the love object of my father, and I could also be
a better husband than Mr. K to get revenge on him. I looked at
him for a long minute. Was he out of his god damned mind? There
was so much in my mind that I couldn't say a word. I stopped
talking altogether and started writing. I began writing to Francis
Bacon the painter. I am going to write a letter everyday and never
speak again to this pukey world. I am going to write across the
threshold of death into his images, because I understand from my
long and happy life that desire is religion, not the desire toward
stupid, human sex but the desire taking us all so far past human
that our faces smudge into dream. I am going to write a love letter
that is irrepressible.

*the first dream was that a house was on fire. My father was
standing beside my bed and woke me up. I dressed myself quickly. Mother
wanted to stop and save her jewel-case filled with pills; but Father said,
"I refuse to let myself and my two children be burnt for the sake of your
jewel-case." We hurried downstairs, and as soon as I was outside I woke
up.*

*the second dream was that I was walking around in a city not
Seattle, but some other city that I did not know and knew at the same time.
Then I came to the apartment where I lived, went to my room, and found
a letter from my mother there. She wrote saying that as I had left home
without my parent's knowledge she had not wished to write to me to say
that my father was so ill that he finally died. She wrote, "now he is dead,
and if you like, you can come." I went to the station and asked about a*

189

hundred times, *"where is the station?"* I always got the same answer: *"Five minutes."* Then I saw a thick wood ahead of me which I went into. All the trees were bodies and all the bodies were trees, and I began to bleed into the darkness of the wood, and I began to feel my body turn into bark and branches and the scars of bark-skin, and I could see mother and the others at the cemetery already as we closed the wood into prayer.

I understand my father and mother very well. I wish I could show them how to be happy instead of submerged. I don't have any questions about their behavior, I see that they are moving the machine of the world, father, mother, daughter, house.

pearly drops bubble up and dribble a bit from the first tear into the flesh of my belly. I found a piece of obsidian and we are on the roof. I make a speckled line of pearly drops and the night presses us flat and her eyes take it all in, unflinching. We love each other like that for ten days straight. We are the new stars come up from the deep bellies of The Den stretching up to meet the heavens. We will drown the sound of the city and the sense of the world of our fathers and mothers out with the sound of The Cure and the prick of a needle meeting its long, outstretched, blue wait.

what is farther? The Algeria I never learn about every day that I actually go to school, or the Obsidian that cuts open history into a wound that won't sew up? We press our wounds together like laughs that go violent and mad. What is farther, the history of the Second World War, or the televised, new and improved productions of a-war-a-week? Obsidian and I can speak French and German to each other. What is farther, the distance between genes, or the long hard ache of wanting to be unborn from this life? I cut therefore I am. Let them eat the cake of a world gone dead so long ago even reading about it in books is nursery rhymes. Why is anyone bothering to try and convince us of history, of geography, of politics? The Den is the World, writing to Francis Bacon is the World, Obsidian and Greta and Michael are the whole globe spiraling toward a USA still trying to teach its children well. What is farther? what is farther, what is father.

the way she turns distills the night into sweet drink so wet it outrains the rain, so black it makes the night into shadow. I tell her I want it more than anything in the world and she forgives me. She traces a beautiful circle around each breast with the obsidian. The red circles don't tell. That's when it happens, my mother comes up on the roof. She's never been up on the roof before in her life, she doesn't want to know about anything, she wants a fuzzy bubble of nothing surrounding her at all times. She wants to be reflexive with objects. But this one time she comes, and her mouth is shaped in the "O" of a mother horrified, a great circle of gasp.

Now comes the choice of what to say. Here is where all parents fail their children. I tell her what she wants to hear, I tell her I have a drug problem, that me and Dana—just like a lie you would tell a man—me and Dana are so high we don't know what we are doing. You know, it all comes down to a question of stories, believable plots, climactic scenes, the pathos of a face—Glenn Close in *Les Liasons Dangereux*, or Greta Garbo, Marlena Dietrich, Robert DeNiro. She buys it. She knows how to play the hysteric.

It is very dark up there on the roof. Light enough for her to see that we have cut around my breasts, dark enough for her to miss the scars that cover my body like white down feathers. For now, it is enough for her to move into her motherhood. She wants the K's out of the house. She wants me to stay home every day for a month. She wants me to see a medical doctor along with the shrink. She has a woman who she thinks is named Dana, a woman who speaks to her only in French, arrested. It all makes such sense. What a logic. No wonder we have Presidents and commercial breaks. No wonder we actually watch the weathermen doing their little soft-shoes around maps of the country.

I found out a week later that Obsidian is OK. She tells Greta and everyone at The Den, "I am loving dora for the tenth day, for the eleventh day, for the twelfth..." She scrapes white marks into the walls to mark the time. She thinks the story of poor dora's craziness is the funniest thing she has ever heard.

Inside I feign illness perfectly, she wonders about infections. I can do this for as long as it takes. I can let my hair go back to its daughter color, I can eat vitamins and watch TV, just like a teen. I can sit at the card table and pretend we are all getting well while the gray days and black nights suck the color out of the rooms, out of the streets, out of the flesh of the world. With us kids these days, it's as easy as breathing to fake a life. I wonder if my father will make it though. He's never dealt well with hysterical women. And I think he needs the sex.

THE DEN

The grain of the wood to the door has the look of a skin weathered by the fall of realities. In 1968, a bar open to the arms of men in the arms of men. A small radius of gentle for a few blocks, the cover of night, a place to sit and drink and be with a man. In 1975, a discotheque, a contest every Thursday night. Rhinestones and sequins and mascara and platinum blondes singing Streisand and Garland and walking the walks. In 1985 a small shift. The music, a bit deeper into the spine, a bit duller ache resonating. Shackles installed against one wall. Two stone pillars with ropes. And a chair, a throne, red velveteen and deep black arms bent back into a slow recline, into a lean beyond pleasure. And a leg rest for each quivering leg spread apart just so. And pillows all around the floor surrounding the chair like so many adoring pets. In a time when sex could send a man behind bars or bloody his face, bruise his bones, The Den held each man tender and warm. In a time when sex became lethal, killing every other member every other week, The Den was reinventing intimacies with each drop of the sun into cover of dark imagining.

A deep amber touches like hands cupped open toward the visitor. This is the back door, through which those coming home enter and re-enter the womb of their new lives. On this side of the door there is an office; a desk, bookshelves, photographs. Marlene Dietrich, Marilyn Monroe, Betty Davis, Barbara Streisand, James Dean, Billy Holiday, and Greta. Greta's books hang like whispers buffering the room against the outside. Rimbaud, Whitman,

Baudelaire, Whitman, Artaud, Virginia Woolf, Gertrude Stein, Swineburn, Oscar Wilde: "The suspense is killing me; I hope it lasts." Words are worlds taking a soul back to itself, taking a soul back into the indifferentiated art of madness, of inside out, of motherloving life. Truman Capote, Andy Warhol, Robert Mapelthorpe. What a different lexicon stacks here. What a clean difference. On the wall too: Madonna next to Madonna and child. On the desk open, Michaelangelo. Michael sitting, fingering, loving the turn from page to page. Greta, watching, loving the gesture of the hand over and over.

But it is on the other side of the door that the oxygen translates heavy air into thick sweet, sweat, dream version of the inside of flesh. Every night at 9:00 she wears it. Every night. Every night she wears it, the room on the other side of the door dresses her black velvet gown and glowing hues of almost lights blinking on and off in red to blue to yellow to red and red and red. The door pulses its heartbeat. In small groups they enter and cluster until the room is a beehive and the honey thickens the walls, the floor, the minds ready and waiting to lose themselves out of the wrong world into the night of this room.

Leather armbands, leather pants, leather chaps and chokers studded with rhinestones or metal. Pierced flesh, the nose, the eyebrow, the lip, the lips. Nipples dripping silver rings and chains, glittering their tiny rain. Shaved heads and bare heads and scarred tattooed immaculates. Bring your lover on a leash or take your turn kneeling or whipping, loving, tenderest touchings in the world. Where else could a body go to be taken care of in a world fixed on hygiene, on incarceration, on smoking laws? In the grocery store one can find pantyhose crinkled up into a ball inside a Styrofoam egg. Where else could a body go?

The Den does not save lives. Inside, they are bredding imagination back up through the cement membrane of a concrete death mask, they are learning to breathe through the pollution of deodorized living, they are re-membering bodies to the point of death. Suffer the children.

Donna Ratajczak

Donna Ratajczak is the author of *The World at My Fingertips* and *Travelog*, short pieces individaully published by Purgatory Pie Press. Her stories and poems have appeared in *Between C & D, A Sheep on the Bus,* and *Zone.* She recently traveled around Japan and China on a research trip for her novel-in-progress, *Never Far From Baltimore.*

Big Grandma Stories

Every morning, Big Grandma braided Debra's hair like she was conquering sin. She laid her weapons out on the kitchen counter: pink plastic brush with black bristles, comb with fat and skinny sets of teeth, bobby pins, rubber bands, shiny satin ribbons. Big Grandma would tell Debra stories as they stood back to belly by the sink. Debra would listen, still and quiet, while her hair got organized. Those were the rules. Debra stared straight ahead where she was pointed; the plastic brush was also good for whacking somebody on the skull.

Spy Priest

Back in the old country, years back, there was a smart priest. Now all priests is smart, and all priests is good, don't take me wrong way. But this priest was specially good and smart. He liked to test people to find out who was weak, and teach them a lesson. He taught many a person a lesson, this good priest. He was very good but strict.

This priest used to put on how you call it? Disguise. He made out he was different things, a milkman, a farmer. He put on those kind of clothes instead of his priest clothes. He did this so he could test people, and see who was good and who was bad. If you see a priest, you try to act good, right? Everybody act good if they see a priest. But if they think it's milkman, or farmer, they act how they act all the time. And this smart priest, if he catch a person doin somethin bad, he would correct them.

One day the priest made out he was a school bus driver. He picked up all the school children like usual. He picked up one child, another child, another child. He pick up every child. He's got a list of them, where they live. Finally, all them children is on the bus. What do you think the priest does?

No. He doesn't take them to school. He stops the bus.

Say what?
No, dummy. He's not out of gas. You wanna be smart aleck. I'll show you smart aleck...

You gonna listen? OK. The priest stops the bus and tells every-body who he really is, a priest. He says to the children: NONE OF YOU CHILDREN ASKED ME WHO I WAS. NONE OF YOU QUESTIONED ME, A STRANGER, DRIVING YOUR BUS. I COULD HAVE BEEN ANYONE. NOW THANK GOD I'M NOT SOME CRAZY PERSON. What do you think he does next?

No, this is not a time to pray the rosary. This was the time for the priest to teach those children a lesson. So the priest takes out this stick he always carries. He takes the stick and he beats all them children that was on that bus.

Hold still...

One day this priest I was tellin you about got the idea to go to a dance at a parish, not his parish, a different one. He wants to see how people act at the dance. Instead of his priest clothes he puts on a nice suit how the people dress them days. He has a nice suit and tie and puts a nice hat on his head. He's a good lookin fella, this priest. He figures no one will recognize he's priest.

So priest is at the dance, makin out he's a regular feller. The way he dress up, he fool everybody. Not one person suspect he's priest. He watches the people and everything they do, so he can see what's going on in this world. He sees people from his parish. They think he's just another feller. He's young, this priest.

He dances with all the girls from his parish, one by one. Just to see how they behave themself. He stands too close to them, you know what I mean? He makes out like he wants to love them up. He's just pretending he's gonna do this. He's priest. He wants to see how these girls react, if they're good girls or not.

What? How he — I don't know when he learned how to dance, that's not part of this story. You gonna be a smart aleck today like yesterday? Shall I teach you another lesson? Don't move your head!

OK, this priest is at the dance. Everybody could dance nice in them days, not like today, that wild carryin on I seen on TV, the girls have no shame. Like wild animal.
Priest dance with one girl, he gets too close, she says to him. "Oh, I'm sorry sir, I think you better find another kind of girl." The priest think, good. And he try the next girl. Same thing. She says, "Could you stand further back, I'm a good Catholic girl." The priest think, good, and he thank her for the dance.

Then he dance with one girl, she act different. When he gets up close like he's gonna make up to her, she don't say nothing. She lets him go on. So they dance for little while, and priest says, "Young lady, you wanna go stand outside?" and the girl goes right along. Well, the priest knows what kind of girl this is. Outside, he tells her who he is. No, of course he don't beat her, he don't have to. He says, HERE I AM, A STRANGE MAN, AND YOU WERE GONNA LET ME SLOBBER ALL OVER YOU IN PUBLIC. YOU SHOULD THANK GOD I WAS PRIEST, TRYING TO TEACH YOU LESSON. And he talks to her about some things you don't need to know nothin about yet. Never

197

mind what. You'll find out when the time come.

He takes that girl back to the church, and he hears her confession right there. I think maybe she has many a sad story to tell. But after long, long confession, the priest blesses her and tells her to go home. You know the best part of this story? After that night, this girl goes into the convent, she becomes a nun. People talk about her all over the place because of her good works that she does helpin people. Years pass, she becomes the mother superior of the convent!

This was all because of the good priest I'm tellin you about.

The Good Father

Long ago not here but in the old country there live this man and his son. The man was a good father, taught his son many things. The father had a shop he made those thing...for horses foot....shoe horse. What? Horseshoe, OK. This man and his son they walk down the road to the town every morning. That's what people did them days. They walk everywhere they wanna go.

Keep your head straight like I put it!

This old man one day decide, "I'm gonna test my son." The next day before they go to town, the man fill his pocket with penny. Then, the man walk a little faster, down the road. When his son ain't lookin, he drop a penny in the road. The boy comes along and sees it. He get excited, he says LOOK FATHER, A PENNY! The father says GOOD! GO AHEAD AND PICK IT UP, SON. Little further on, the son ain't lookin, the father drop another penny. The son says I FOUND ANOTHER PENNY! Every time the father says GOOD! GO AHEAD AND PICK IT UP, SON. The son don't miss one penny.

The next time they go to the town, the father's got cherries in his pocket. He drop them on the ground like the last time, when the son ain't watchin. And the son says LOOK FATHER, A CHERRY! I FOUND A CHERRY! I FOUND ANOTHER CHERRY! And the father says, GOOD SON. EAT THE CHERRY. As fast as the father drop the cherry, the son eat them. *Course he don't know* the father drop the cherry. The father don't let on, he just say, GOOD.

The next day the father and son walk to town. This time the father carry nails in his pocket, like for shoe on a horse. Oh, how you call that thing? What? Horseshoe, OK. That's what the nails is for in his pocket. They nail the shoe on the horse. So the father carry these kind of nail along. He throw them out when the son wasn't lookin, like before. Only this time the son don't pick them up. He just keep walkin along behind his father, so busy thinkin about penny or cherry he can't see nothin else.

When they get to town, the father take his son aside. He show him a nail. The father say WHAT IS THIS, SON. The boy say, A NAIL, FATHER. And the father say, YOU DIDN'T SEE THIS IN THE ROAD? The boy says NO, FATHER. The father explain, I PUT PENNY, I PUT CHERRY, I PUT NAIL. YOU PICK UP THE PENNY, YOU PICK UP THE CHERRY, BUT YOU LEFT ALL THEM NAILS LAY THERE. And the father gets a stick, and beat the boy.

Keep your head straight, let me put ribbon.

Debra stared at her reflection in the dining room mirror. A strange girl with handles sticking out of her head stared back.

Jardine Raven Libaire

Jardine Raven Libaire, winner of the 1995 Glasscock Award, has poetry published in *Whiskey Island Magazine*, *Valley Women's Voice*, *Riverrun*, *Mobius*, and other literary magazines. She lives in Ann Arbor, Michigan.

Revolution

February

The powder-blue carpet in the hallway pushes against walls that flake like stale eggs. I'm following the American exchange student to her bedroom.

"It's a bubblegum tree," she says.

"Really?" I ask.

She puts her new plant down on the desk in a mess of air mail envelopes.

"No, they're little roses or something. I paid eighty francs for it at the corner florist."

It's an act of submission to speak someone else's language. I don't think we've had a single conversation in French since she moved in here.

The long window behind her is open and my hands feel vitally connected to the doves outside; I would like to be a white bird fluttering between her thighs, moving up and down, then folding my wings to die.

The American has seduced the family. Father drops bread in the lap of his Hugo Boss suit and Mother flushes. The American is allowed to leave wedges of Roquefort and a single potato on her plate; the rest of the plates are licked clean, or else. She shifts lewdly in her chair. The girl takes ballet, as a joke. She claims that she's no ballerina and that her instructor at Paris Centre is abusive. But she laughs about all of this. The family is afraid to meet her half-lidded aquamarine eyes.

When I walked in on her this morning, she was in pink tights and black leotard. The room smelled of hashish, but I said nothing. My silence allowed me to watch, from the application of black eyeliner to blue eyeshadow, and lastly, the wide ruby lips, pouting and waiting to be bitten. The doves on the iron balcony joined me and we formed a strange audience.

Today Mother went into the girl's room and found her lying on the bed, sweating whiskey. Mother gave her a volume of Baudelaire because the girl had mentioned something, and since we wait on her hand and foot. So early in the evening, before dinner, the blood red sun still in the Arc de Triomphe, Father not home yet from the bank, and the girl is drunk.

The whole family knows she takes things from the kitchen in the middle of the night, bowls of Muselix, gateau chocolat, but no one dare say a thing. Today I came up from behind when she was washing blood stains from her underwear in the sink. You can imagine; I backed away slowly, taking my shadow with me.

Even though it's pointless, I try to decipher my feelings for her. Twice in a row I dreamed of her as a black dog, rubbing her silky head under my hand.
Someone took her to dinner last night and she showed up this morning in her white silk dress with a new flask. She showed me the silver flask, engraved JLH, with love, BBS. And the date. She simultaneously watered the pink bubblegum plant and un-strapped her black heels.

I sleep in the room next to hers. I can sometimes feel a tremble in the wall dividing our beds and I'm sure she's masturbating. In the silence after, her pink-rimmed eyes must twitch as she falls directly asleep with her fist full of honey.
Her whole presence takes up the room with sleep at night. The black void is filled with nightmares and with her ivory limbs folded during the REM phase. I imagine that the flutter of her eyelids must match the pulse of blood down to my groin. I feel like

I'm taking advantage of her sleep to imagine her (and to imagine and imagine her) motionless.

I blame it on the blood racing into my groin. And I blame the blood on the woman in her chamber, perfume of gardenia on her ankles, cherry lips.

We know she urinates in her bidet. It's one of those things we pretend not to know, but there's an aftersmell that's incriminating around noontime.

March
During the night, her own hands find herself, but unlike the pure hyacinth that used to bloom there, releasing a fragrance that comes under the door and out into the hall, she feels something darker. I can see through the wall as if it was glass; a bat clawing its oily way into her.

Mornings, she walks through the rain with her mahogany-handled, green silk umbrella. Her pale hands are omens of delicacy to all the trench-coated businessmen. Her hands promise the gentle way a saint would cut a pheasant's throat.

Mother's working on an apple, maneuvering the knife as if she was skinning someone's heart.
"She's not a lady."
I sigh because I see where things are going. I wander around the house, studying the mildew patterns in the wallpaper. Rain comes down on the motorcycles lined up beneath the front balcony.
I find the American watching our black-and-white TV, a documentary on French prisons. Something silver caught in her lashes.

At night, she goes back and forth. I hear her plunge into the chlorine pool of sleep and then drag herself out, eyes stinging. She's rocking dangerously, in fear of her luminous curtains, pulled down by her dreams, waking up with something silver in her lashes.

She comes home from Le Casbah this morning. Her jaw's clamped shut but she manages to tell me some story: her friend Molly back from Amsterdam, bobby socks full of speed, a greasy, black train coming to Paris from Amsterdam.

I feel the heaviness at night. I hear her flip through the pages of *Vogue*, frosted lips and silver nipples. She turns the glossy pages frantically, but then I hear the bat descend, taking her thighs in his cartilaged wings.

Tuesday morning, she's white-nightgowned. She points to the wall where she's taped up pictures of Ferraris, a 246 Dino, a 330 GTC.
"Vroom-vroom," she says.
Wednesday, she stands on a chair in a shaft of dusty light. She's wearing her robin's egg blue bikini.
"Should I go to Marseilles tomorrow?"
There are ghosts in this room, pockets of air that smell like rotting fruit. Neither of us should ignore them, but we do.

Friday my parents went to the opera. Tonight they're having a cocktail party for people from the bank and they have asked the American to find somewhere else to be. They asked her over breakfast, over octagonal slices of clementine.

She has an ivory, blue-veined throat that is wrapped today in a wine-colored scarf. Mother is arranging forsythia branches when the girl walks into the foyer, rain dripping off her sleeves. They meet, stone eye to stone eye.
"What are you doing?" the girl asks.

"I'm forcing them."

Father over leg of lamb and watercress inquires about her education. There's a mumbled history of elementary experience, art studios, field hockey and jewelry workshops.

As always, Mother finds a discrepancy.

"Well, actually," the girl says. "I went to two different boarding schools. I was expelled from the first one."

Father doesn't understand.

"It was the hierarchy," she explains. "It's the way things like that work."

She says this mechanically, the way she'd play a piano exercise that she learned as a blonde, bruised child growing up in Central Islip, Long Island, New York, in the United States of America.

I think she's sick. She's up and down the blue carpet to the bathroom. When she pulls the chain to flush, doves take off from the roof.

The girl's also gained weight; the back of her thighs below the pink velour skirt are cellulite.

The night before she told me her story was particularly dark, no moon, late dawn. I knew she was awake the whole time, though. I could hear her clipping her toenails and smoking her Newports.

The Girl's Story

Her brass doorknob turns easily. The house is deaf now, my parents' white ears crushed in platonic sleep. But I've been listening to the girl for hours, spilling pills into the bidet, cursing as she fishes them out, pacing. When I walk in, she's flossing her teeth, her eyes almost swollen shut.

When she sees me, she starts to cry again, white thread hanging from between her front teeth.

I touch her shoulder.

"What's wrong?"
"I don't know."
"You can tell me."
"No, no, no—"
Sobbing.

When it's more calm:
"I don't think you like me," she whispers.
Silence.
"Why don't you tell me what's wrong?" I ask.
"I wouldn't know where to start."
"Start at the worst part."

Across the street, a light goes on in a kitchen. The yellow square holds a woman in a maroon robe.

"The worst part.
"It started in November one year. I had a scab on my lip from getting hit in field hockey..."
"Was it getting cold?"
"Oh, sure, it was getting cold. And then the snow fell mid-November."
Her heartbeat makes the nightgown tremble where the monogram falls, JLH, right below the collarbone.
"Blazing morning that turned the snow pink. I had a fever; I waited in the infirmary with Andrew Ashton who I had given a hand job to the week before in the choir loft."

For a while I think she's fallen asleep, her head heavy as lead.

"So I spent the first few days in there alone. My aunt and uncle from the city sent me balloons. I had mono—did I say I had mono? I did nothing but sleep. I didn't even dream. Nothing. When I did wake up once, there was Penelope.

"Lower-mid. I was an upper-mid. Scandinavian, real blonde. She slept, too. We slept for weeks and the snow kept coming down.

"Nothing to do when we did wake up. This little transistor radio.

"Welkin and Roy made us change our nightgowns once a day and they took our temperatures.

"If I have faraway eyes, then Penelope has close-up ones, if you know what I mean.

"Lot of snow that year."

Her eyes are half moons in the dark and they keep tipping back into her head until she wakes with a start.

"So it was Penelope's birthday, which she almost forgot until Nurse Roy brought in a pink cake. We sang with the lights off, candles golden and shining on Roy's white cap.

"They liked us, I think, Penelope especially. The way her tongue would peek out between her teeth when she was doing a crossword.

"And then, and I don't want to gross you out or anything, because it's hard to explain. I mean that I liked it, too, when she touched her tongue to my mouth that night, with the infirmary lights off and Welkin watching the late-night movie. We spooned, her stomach to my back, like twins in identical nightgowns.

"Does this bother you?" Very upset. Gulping like something might come up from her stomach.

"The worst part.

"Early January?

"Still lots of snow. Woke up some mornings to the sound of deerhunters in the snow, or hockey players coming back from pre-dawn practice at the town rink.

"This particular morning I woke up with Penelope laughing

207

and poking me in the ribs. 'It's asleep in the radiator,' she whispered. 'Do something, Jean. Get it.' And she was right. A bat was sleeping in between the pipes of the radiator, leather wings folded.

"We didn't kill it; it wasn't us. It was Welkin. The whole thing was kind of exciting until then, until Welkin came in with a tennis racquet that they kept in the janitor's closet for this reason. She poked around the radiator, her big ass in my face.

"I saw a wing move. And then it was terrible; the bat hit the ceiling, the window, got caught in the curtains. All the time squealing and Welkin was slamming it with the racquet.

"It ended up on Penelope's bed, a dark skin with a tiny face.

"That afternoon was when I first held Penelope in the daylight, saw exactly how fragile her ribcage was.

"It was that afternoon when Welkin stood in the doorway and watched me lick the tears off Penelope's cheeks, my arm around her narrow waist and hers around mine.

"And then they hated us."

I am looking at a blue band that has appeared through Paris. Dawn? Already? I realize she's crying again, hiccuping. Her feverish face is beautiful and flushed. I want to do something. I don't know, I'm tired. I have crazy thoughts.

But then the girl saves me and saves us both.

"Uh-oh."

So instead I spend the early part of the morning with her on her knees over the toilet, saying:

"That's right. Get it out.

"You just have to get it out of your system."

April

For a week or so, things run like a factory. The girl empties Mother's bags of fruit from the market, lifting each kiwi like it is a hairy egg. She has a dumb smile on her face.

She no longer looks me in the eye.

Her weekend in Bologna included a party at a Communist-occupied building of the university. She comes back with burgundy go-go boots and a silver-blue box of Bacci chocolates for the family.

Some days she stays in bed, a Diet Coke can between her knees. I stand in the doorway and watch her as she looks away into the liquid blue above Paris.

Of course she's going to move. The girl sets up an appointment with the director of the program, who comes to tea with her bulldog on a leash. During the meeting the bulldog laps at a saucer of sugarmilk, Mother signs papers, and the American breathes evenly, bloodshot eyes locked on the sky.

Mother spends a day or two vacuuming and polishing. Crawling around the room on her bony knees, she collects hairballs. She finds a rotting tangerine beneath the bed.

At night I sometimes think I hear the girl feeling her way down the hall, trying to find her own room. I imagine her fiddling with the shark's tooth around her neck at dinner. And I remember her leaving and how I thought, I can do something, right now. Right Now.

My friend says she works at Chez George, so I go by to see. I stand behind a maroon Mercedes and watch her through the window, watch the bartender arrange tiger lilies. I feel like I'm watching a silent movie as white tablecloths float down from the American's fingertips, the sheets drifting down in slow motion. She moves around the room in a seemingly haphazard fashion, but I know her better than that by now.

I know that she lives by a different order.

Lou Robinson

Lou Robinson is the author of *Napoleon's Mare*, a novel. Her work has appeared in *The American Voice, The Kenyon Review, Quarterly, Epoch, Black Ice*, and in the anthologies*Top Top Stories* (City Lights Press) and *Transgressions* (The University of Iowa Press). *Surveillance*, a collaboration with Ellen Zweig, was published on the WWW by *CTheory*.

Splendid Protectors

There are no innocent bystanders. What were
they doing there in the first place?
—*William Burroughs*

A falling window box struck and killed a woman walking down
Hudson Street. Where was her gros bon ange? Six stories above
her innocent head, Sylvia had been standing out on the box to
photograph her pansies. She rode the box to the ground where the
other body cushioned her strike. Sylvia survived and may recover
completely or not. Now she is wheeled around by her constant
keeper. The dead woman's purse burst spewing a bag of M & M's
into a puddle of water left by Sylvia's watering can, where they
floated, green, red, brown, and that hideous tan. Box, purse,
water, angel, almost every thing at some time has stood for a
woman. No thing is ever innocent.

Protection is often lifted, they tell me. They said I had to be
removed. I was always at the ready, looking up at something
falling. But maybe they merely meant removed from her path.
Sylvia had fallen in love with someone else and moved to the city,
several months before her spectacular fall. My splendid protec-
tors. Splendid once was a verb, said my friend Susan, as in the way
Loretta Young splended through the doorway. Her skirt always
twirled enough. Depraved another. As in she depraved herself.

After I was removed, I lay on the lawn chair in Susan's
orchard counting my losses. Something shot me in the forehead.
Had Sylvia hired an assassin? It would not be unlike her at all to
blame me for not having been there to catch her. An apple
bounced to the ground. That was Saturn passing, I hoped, in vain.
In a drawer upstairs I had just read that a six-ounce object

involved in a typical 5-mile-per-second collision in a low-Earth orbit would hit with the force of an 8-ton truck moving at 97 mph.

They said this particular juxtaposition, Saturn, Pluto, my poor moon, would never come again, unless I lived to 104. During its transit, all will be stripped away, as if there is no ground, as if there never was. The stony lane, the sleeping hay, the queen Anne's lace, the watery blue-green door, the sleeping cat loft, the vodka gimlet porch swing—I never really lived there with her. Her heat stretched against me, her morning coffee and milk breath, the proud plain of her freckled chest, it never really happened. I never expected to grow old with someone named Sylvia. I never really believed.

Don't dally to gather shards, they said. When you sep a rate, the once-warm flood of feelings solidifies into objects that demand attention. This chest of drawers, that mirror, those snow tires that only saw one upstate winter. Run, abandon everything. Pretend your personality is still a mobile liquid contained within your skin. It is a brittle, breakable thing inseparable from the world, but use your imagination. "The world is made up of things," Sylvia said scornfully. And, "You should get your things out as quickly as possible."

They told me, You are like a marble in a maze. Close your eyes, lie back, roll out. Other arms will catch you.

Other arms. They said to think about touch. The cruelest thing they ever said. When I know about the other arms holding her? That? Now?

Yes. Whatever is hardest to imagine is best done fast, lest one slide into paralysis, having thought of it. Into victimdom, having feared it.

Touch is my kingdom, I shall not want.

One year previous I held my dying horse's head in my lap, in a stall on top of Bald Mountain. Breath holds matter up and then leaving, leadens it. The dead horse, Fiddle, can only be summoned by the memory of feel. His curved, warm, one-eighth Percheron neck and the deep, oily, enveloping mane. The hot, soft, seven-eighths Arab breath that was his speech, saying "You're here! You're mine," or "Make your meaning clear! Take your stand."

Is it possible to think about the feel of the place there under Sylvia's hair with an intensity of focus that freezes pain, the same way studying color has often staved off disintegration? Splendid color. My dead horse's coat was copper, bittersweet. The apple missile is pale, green-streaked pink, chalky on the teeth. Biting a pastel crayon, biting off the tip of that friend's mother's mulberry lipstick. No, it isn't. Splendid is a depraved word, cynical, pulling you down into its beautiful arms.

They said to study false sensation, also. A year before my horse died I was hit by a car. I thought only, can I still ride? I ran my mind down each limb. Later I argued with the doctor about whether or not I had hit my head, since I couldn't remember feeling it. Twenty-two stitches above the left eyebrow. A long narrow room of confusion ensued, conviction a fist under the sternum that opened and clenched and opened and leaked. Previous assumptions mocked and abandoned me. They said *Sometimes violence is necessary to make an opening for change.* Fuckheads.

During my recuperation, I became convinced that if I didn't clean Fiddle's sheath right away he would die of prostate cancer. All over the house I left scraps of paper saying "ssheath" so I wouldn't forget. Under that they said "sunglassses" because mine lay shattered in the floor of the car with no ceiling. S's were trouble. Double s's were downright sinister and had to become three. Three, ha, little did I know.

Out in the pasture by the road, my head swathed in bandages, I struggled to pull out his penis. In the tip of the urethra is a hard little concretion of smegma called the bean that must be removed. Finally I had it, a pale rock exactly like a navy bean, very satisfying to hold. Beyond us a row of cars had stopped along the highway.

It wasn't the bean that killed him. A parasite, a mysterious

protozoa, invaded his blood, moving slowly into his spine, sometimes straddling a nerve, sometimes lying in wait. First he lost
touch with the ground. One morning my horse would be strutting,
each hoof placed precisely where it showed his magnificence to
most advantage. The next morning. Every other next morning.
Fog, blue-violet hills of Danby State Forest. My horse, looking
off, because at least I had managed to give him the long view,
Arabians need that. Trying to put his hoof where it would hold up
his body, failing to know when it was home on the earth, where it
ended. Falling down, centuries of breeding stumbling over a
weed, over nothing. Loss is neurological, a circuit that can be
interrupted. But only intermittently.

I would have traded her life for my horse's then. There are
no innocents. Pluto taking away the earth from under our feet,
Fiddle's and mine. My Fiddler Fair. How careful he was of his
feet. Jumping over puddles, shadows, brown paper bags blown off
the highway. Jumping over the place where once a brown paper
bag had been and now was missing, despicable deceiving ghost of
bag.

Pure love and squalid. Here with the relics of squandered
care, where the human brand of passion remains intense but
turned toward vengeance, depraved objects refuse to flatten.
Refuse to void themselves of their poison bean. A book of blurry
photos of china horses, the Eddy sweater, English riding boots.
Things she gave me, the ghosts of things she forgot to give back,
things she gave but now doesn't want to pay for. "Stop acting like
a victim," she screamed. Long before she fell.

Then milk the venom from the objects of a life together. See
how mean you can be. On every resumé for every job, Sylvia
included "milked cows in Oregon in 1971." Think of the head-
hunters in their perfect navy suits at the table in the expensive
New York City restaurant where they have flown her to discuss
how she might fit into their plans for the Museum. Think of them
thinking of the cows and her hands around their teats. Think of
the time she came home more famous and said, "I could live

214

anywhere now. What will you do, take your two little weeks vacation to come along?" and "I can't promise I won't sleep with her," and "All you want to do is hang out in a horse barn."
Think of her saying maybe I wasn't a real lesbian. This had to do with an unwillingness to yell and scream. A lesbian manqué? What is a lesbian? Manqué, lacking, sans serif, missing the little tail. Also a tomboy. A lesbian is manqué by definition. Maybe that is what she was screaming about. Meanwhile she pursues her third married woman, from her wheelchair.
Work the mouth with small, gentle circles. Slide the fingers over the gums, work the lips inside and out. One or two sessions will cure the animal of biting and aggression.
They say I don't need more armor. I need more heart, not less. At first I thought they meant love more instead of suffering, puff out the shrunken little organ like a bellows and forgive forgive forgive. Form a shield of compassion, the bright white Christian kind. But Susan said they meant Speed up. Think of Fiddle, his forward surge. If something attacks you, jump sideways if you must, then trot right up to it, touch it, bite or kick it back. Give it a whack, send it rolling.
But they also say my Moon is off on its own, unable to speak easily except to animals. Wonderful hands, a natural seat, my riding teachers always said. Unaspected they call this moon. Like mumbling or having no eyebrows.
My gros bon anges said You have once again let yourself be silenced. Six years ago when I met her they had said You will one day have to walk away.
When you refuse to listen to your gros bon anges, you begin to deprave yourself. My demon guides. Either they poison my path before me or they merely fail to turn my feet. They have four hooves and hair the colors of root beer, coca cola, cognac, licorice.
Late at night in the indoor arena, the lights of the small city pinking up the snow of the pasture through the one open wall, I rode my dead horse bareback. An achievement on a horse who only cared about speed and distance. Who raced trains. Who

always ran for the opening ahead. Who had to be first even in a circle. Making three circles for every other horse's one, in clouds of pink-lit sawdust. Deciding where the circle began and heading for it, then choosing another opening to be the beginning, the winning space, then choosing again.

She was jealous of my dead horse. "It's the same as my having another lover," she insisted.

Will, the farrier, said, "You women. You all think your horse is your lover." I don't, I answered, I think he is God. Will should know this because his first wife was a Blackfoot Indian like my grandmother and they say Pray to Horse; Man has no god but Horse has a god. Will is always trying to cut our hair, he wants to have sex with our hair. He's jealous of women and horses. He's tired of ministering to the feet of gods. He refused to shoe my new horse. He said he couldn't afford to die.

My father's mother, Ida May—long bones, black hair, flat red-orange lipstick—carried a black satchel full of multi-colored pills for her bad moods. As a child in Berea, Kentucky, her stepmother had sent her away to the orphanage from time to time. Ora didn't want "a blackfeet nigger talking that chipmunk talk to the natural kids." My grandmother's papa, Mott, would go get her back. At sixteen she married my grandfather and they ran away to Indiana. He got a job in the firehouse where he could monitor the movements of negras on the police band.

My father spent many summers on Papa Mott's farm. The first Christmas after my father returned from the war, my grandmother asked him for the sheepskin coat he had brought back from Guadal Canal. It had belonged to a marine friend who had died there beside him in a ditch. She and my father drove the coat down to her Papa Mott on the old farm near Berea, along with cornmeal, a chicken, canned ruby beets. Papa Mott was getting weak but wouldn't go to a doctor. His wife had left a bottle of aspirin on the shelf with a note in it, "You can take one of these, they won't hurt you." He hadn't taken one yet. He never had an outhouse; he pissed in the stall with the mule.

When she was nine, my grandmother had a little bulldog. Ora hung it from a tree outside my grandmother's bedroom window.

When my grandfather died, my father said he came home and rode around and around on his Harley, trying to run over the next door neighbor's beagle. "No you didn't" I always said. I didn't believe in the violence of grief. I believed I could heal it. I was grief's sponge.

My new horse is a young half-Belgian, half-Morgan titan who misses his mother. Sometimes his nose will suddenly go long and pointed, rigid, and you should expect something evil. He gives himself away because he can; he knows his mass requires no subterfuge. Then he lunges—rearing, bucking, suspended five feet in the air, an enraged elephant. Loving him is easy and dangerous. You love what can crush you, accidentally, in its terrible innocence. I can afford to die. Your gros bon anges, they move you in and out of trajectories. They have their reasons. So why be shocked. That one day she said she could never live without me and only one day later everything had to end, touch, even speech.

My titan is lame to the right. His left hock suddenly grew a soft pouch like something overripe and cursed under the skin. When you touch it, the little package moves to the other side of his leg. He has to go to the vet lab, but no one can get him in a trailer. The only time he was in one he panicked, tore off its halter, and rode three hours with his head squished to one side. He is a volcano of fear. The steel gate is crushed to one-fourth his size from the first day they turned him out without his mother. Sometimes he becomes hypnotized by an unfamiliar sight. He plants his giant feet and goes away inside his head, shorted out by the conflict between wanting to stay and to flee. His eyes go vague and he can't hear or feel. Then I have to slap him quick all over with flat loud smacks before he leaves his body for good. None of the outcomes are acceptable. All touch is a vanishing. Uranus hangs on the upper right and freezes the hock. The planet is stuck in the transit.

Your hand can't stay long in one place or the place grows numb to sensation. Your hand has to keep traveling. Touch is an instantaneous memory. Sometimes a bitter, unrelenting memory. It is held in the neurons and forever bends the organism away from balance, reason, or release. Any system trapped in periodicity is made chaotic again when nudged at specific points. Stroked or licked or lied to. Or it falls with the velocity of a 14-ton truck.

To isolate the pain, they will block out, one at a time, each part of each leg with anesthetic, then each time make him go around in a circle. So he will trot for a space in a splendid, even rhythm, unaware of the tearing tissue, the chipping bone, the pinching nerve. He always goes when you ask. That's what he's here for.

My tender willing creature. Fifteen hundred pounds. When we come across a smallish strangeness—the smell of hoof oil, a child with a popsickle stick protruding from her mouth, some ice cubes spilled on the bench—he rests his nose by my nose and breaths out softly for reassurance. Stroking his lips soothes him, and murmuring so soft that it is an exhalation rather than a sound. Eating grass in little tugs he grows alarmed and bolts at the sight of a canoe strapped to the roof of a car on the highway. I'm inside his brain now, driving. When I see something flapping I brace myself, I'm ready to fly. Fiddle tried to teach me to stand and fight. This one tells me to leave it behind, swiftly. Whatever it was, it wasn't worth it.

He tugs loose a tall weed, shakes the dirt off the root, chews, gazing off, thinking of things he has lost and things that may hurt him. He is beginning to trust me. He will come to think I can break his fall.

Tristan Taormino

Tristan Taormino is co-founder and owner of Black Dog Productions, a literary agency. She is co-editor of *Best Lesbian Erotica
1996* (Cleis Press), and *Ritual Sex* (Richard Kasak Books), and
editor of *Power Tools* (Masquerade Books). Her work appears in
the anthologies *The Femme Mystique, Heatwave, Women in Love
and Lust, Virgin Territory II, Strategic Sex,* and *While the Dancing
Divas Were Out and About,* as well as *On our Backs, X-X-X Fruit,
Venus Infers,* and *Blue Blood.* She is publisher and Editrix of the
zine *Pucker Up.* She lives in Brooklyn with her dog, Reggie Love.

CAUTION: Sharp Object

Every inch of me is covered in blue saran wrap, and I must be suffocating. The boy in the bed with me has named himself after two American icons, part sex kitten, part serial killer. He might look like a young Alice Cooper if he didn't look so much like Pee-Wee Herman's psycho-sinister twin with long black hair shiny but thirsty from all the dyeing, bright red lips, black ink-drawing tattoos over creamy vampire skin, and dangly girl-fingers encased with sharp silver rings. He looks at me with eyes defined by thick black slashes; I gaze back through the glossy plastic. He's skinny, so skinny he looks like a high school boy in cut-off jeans and he acts like one. This is that young alternative rockerboy who commits perverse acts on stage, fresh from his arrest in Florida for getting naked during a show. Yeah, he knows he's a star, but he's shy with me. (He won't let me see his dick, even though he's going to be naked in the photos.) I am already naked, except for one ripped pink stocking alone on my left thigh, pussy freshly shaved, my black eyeliner and dark red lipstick (to match his) carefully smeared and messed 'til I look like I've been savaged or ravaged, or maybe raped. He covers himself in front of my eyes, innocently twirling the telephone cord. Who is the kitten and who is the killer? He is the boy just interviewed in that music mag where they want to hear about his influences, when he'll be in the studio again, and all he wants to talk about is sex and his obsession with *erotic asphixiation*. He likes to choke girls while he fucks them. The photographer is standing over the bed, checking the light. My tits are too bright. He asks me again if I feel alright, if everything's cool. I say yeah, and he tells me okay, then I'm going to start shooting. Look dead, he says. But keep your eyes open.

I'm full from our three hour dinner; my insides are dripping of pure virgin olive oil, swimming in sweet red wine. I think we're going home, but we're suddenly walking the opposite direction from the car towards *that* street, and then we're walking past the neon lights and windowless walls: xxx live girls nude girls girl-girl sex shows xxx. She knows the place she wants to go, a place where the doorman won't smirk or give us a hard time or yell, "fuckin' dykes!" at us. But I forget we're passing tonight, her in a dark doublebreasted suit, me in my short flowered dress. We're a boy-girl couple looking for adventure. Inside our own private booth, I see her, this girl that's going to dance for us. I wonder if I ever looked that cute perky tired annoyed ready sexy when I danced. I wonder how many times my date has cruised the shows, how many she times has come here to this one, how many times she has seen her, this one. But I don't have time to think all of it through because she's messing with me, rubbing her hands between my legs, pushing the dress up while she watches the dancer wink at her. Does she know she's winking at another girl? Or does she just think it's a handsome man out on a date with a much younger girl. A girl who was asked for i.d. at the door, thought to be sixteen, actually almost twenty-four, but feeling sixteen, like a nyphomaniac teenage girl needing to be fucked all the time. I spread my legs for her. She knows I want it 'cause I always want it—need it—from her. She slides back my wet panties, can't take her eyes off the girl, can't take her hands off me. I'm pretending she's never done this before, never taken a girl here. I close my eyes so they can watch each other and I can watch it all in my head.

The blond is not as girlie as she looks: bleached-out, ratty hair cut in different lengths with intense black roots; pale and perfect skin, slightly flushed to match her soft, pink, fuzzy sweater stretched over touchable breasts; deep brandy-colored lips overdrawn and painted outside the lines; lace-up boots over ripped fishnets. Drinking a martini straight from the chrome shaker. She and her rough-and-tough looking bass player are shooting a threesome. I'm naked again, except for white knee socks and shiny red patent leather Mary Janes. The blond kneels in front of me as if she's about to eat my hairless pussy between spread legs while the bass player stands behind me, holds my arms behind my back and watches. The bass player is shorter, with bright orange hair cut in a shaggy flip, a sort of Tori Spelling-on-speed kind of look. Flashes blind my eyes, and I can't see anything, only hear her in my ear. Telling me how much she likes to ass-fuck girls, girlie girls like me, how perfect my lips are, how fuckable my ass is, how much she wants to stick her tongue up inside me. The blond moves closer to me, and I wonder if these two are lovers. Yes, they certainly could be. They'll go home tonight and fuck, the bass player whispering things to the blond, or the blond will think of eating my cunt while she's eating hers and get off that way. No. The orange haired one sneaks the test prints from the shoot into the bathroom, covers her girlfriend's body and jerks off in the middle of the night to me, my naked body held together by her, spread apart for her lover.

We meet at a club and I'm all dolled up for her in a silver lamé baby doll dress, thigh highs, black high heel lace up boots, and the silver chain collar, locked around my neck since the day she put it there. It's a leatherboy bar, so I'm the only one in a dress, and she likes that, likes it so much that she leads me to the corner bathroom, pushes the door closed, leaving it slightly open and takes her dick out, makes me suck it from on my knees on the cold dirty bathroom floor which smells like piss and cigarettes. I take its length in my mouth as she pushes herself into me, shoving her dick down my throat, so I can feel it scrape the roof of my mouth. There's lipstick on the condom when she pulls herself out of me and lifts me up on the sink facing her, so she can kiss me, bite my lips, suck on my neck. She tastes like smoke and beer. I'm not wearing any underwear she discovers, as she lifts my skirt up to see what's hers. I'm slick and swollen and my legs and lips are spread for her. She rubs herself at my opening, presses the head into my clit, pushes there as I steady myself on the tiny sink. I know that there are boys right outside, peering through the six inch space, growing hard in their denim and leather, stroking themsleves at the sight of such a capable top with such a big dick. I'm sure they all want her to fuck them and make them suck her, but I'm daddy's little girl and all they can do is peek through the opening and listen through the door and imagine. I can see the whole scene in the filthy mirror on the back of the door. Behind the door, their eyes and their bulges are watching me.

He looks like a freak: straggly brown hair, deep set eyes no describable color, and a wizened apple head face, incredible lines marking the flesh of his now-kicked heroin habit, late nights cutting himself on stage, touring and trashing the clubs he's played in. I've tied him to a chair with thick black rope, the cameras are rolling, a song I've never heard before is playing really loud. He's talking, saying some shit about how nice my tits are, how he wants to eat my pussy, and I don't want him to talk anymore. I want him to shut that smart mouth of his, shut the fuck up, so I slap him as hard as my hand will let me. While his skin is still stinging, I pry his fat, stupid mouth open and shove a flourescent ball gag in there. I buckle the leather strap too tight around his head and make sure to get some little pieces of hair caught in it, so he winces and struggles. Then it begins, my favorite part. Saliva runs down his chin, neck and chest. He is salivating like the dog he is, drooling uncontrollably like the sick freak he is. He needs to be smacked, fuck it, he wants to be, but most importantly, I want to pound his face until he cries. Each black leather lash of the whip is braided with knotted ends. I begin slowly, establish a rhythm that will falsely lull him as I beat his chest, and when I feel like it, I move my arm just slightly, so that a few lashes graze his neck and if he flinches they will hit his face, wet with spit. I know it hurts, I can see the red welts raising up on his skin, and he can't scream or ask me to stop or tell me to.

His eyes plead with me. He's asking for it. I'm high from fucking this mother-fucker and if someone yelled cut or stop, I didn't hear it.

When I come home from a long shoot, she's got her dick on and the lights off. She's jerking off to the glow of a porn movie with her cock in one hand and the remote in the other, watching this big blond guy sodomize her favorite brunette. I know I'm next. She takes her eyes off the screen for a moment to watch me put my stuff down and strip. I kiss her. She says I smell like plastic and darkroom chemicals. She tells me I'm a slut, *dirty*, and I better scrub my body good, get all the sleaze off me, because she's not going to touch me until all the makeup is off, the marks of a day's work are gone, and I'm fresh and clean and *hers* again. She wants to watch me do it, but she wants to watch the action on the screen more. So I go to the dark room alone, and I'm glad she has let me because I need the solitude, the hot water, the sound of it flooding the bathtub. When I climb in, the water scorches my skin, but I like to feel the stings in the places I've been hit, the aches of the muscles I've strained. I want to look at my skin wet and flushed, feel my pussy under my hand as I jerk off, but there will be a knock at the door soon. And when the lights come on, I'll be ready to dance for her again.